ONLY

CROS

WILL CARSTON: Years of hard riding as a Ranger and of peacekeeping as a wartime town marshal taught him one lesson: You can't stop a good man in the right . . .

WASH CARSTON: In the Civil War he fought for the Confederate flag until the last surrender. Now Will Carston's youngest son won't endure defeat again . . .

CHANCE CARSTON: His hair-trigger temper often got him in trouble—especially in a country where a man who'd worn the Union blue wasn't always welcome. But in the showdown coming violent and fast, he'd risk his life for his father and brother . . .

BEN THOMPSON: A crack shot with a secret past, he volunteered to ride with the Carstons. The frontiersman was easy to like, and hard to trust . . .

JACK TERRENCE: He was a strong man with lots of guts in a tight spot. But the young renegade couldn't stand up to his own father . . .

VEGAS: A quick-talking outlaw who used the law to his advantage, he relied on his well-armed thugs when it came time to battle the Carstons . . .

ONCE THE FOOLISH AND
THE BRAVE
CROSS AN EX-RANGER!

Books By Jim Miller

Ranger's Revenge
The Long Rope

Published by POCKET BOOKS

THE LONG ROPE

JIM MILLER

POCKET BOOKS

New York London Toronto Sydney Tokyo Singapore

An *Original* Publication of POCKET BOOKS

POCKET BOOKS, a division of Simon & Schuster Inc.
1230 Avenue of the Americas, New York, NY 10020

ISBN: 0-671-66947-8

First Pocket Books printing September 1990

10 9 8 7 6 5 4 3 2 1

POCKET and colophon are registered trademarks of Simon & Schuster Inc.

Printed in the U.S.A

This one is for Donald Williams Collins.
Both of them.
If I could only teach the one
As well as I was taught by the other.

CHAPTER

★ 1 ★

What in the hell is that?" I asked, peering off into the distance. What had gotten my attention was the gathering of dust on the horizon. Hell, I hadn't seen that much in one place since the last time we'd found enough flat ground to fight on during the war, and that wasn't that long ago.

"Comanche?" my brother asked, a suddenly worried look on his face.

"No, I doubt it." I wiped away the sweat from my forehead. It was July of 1865 and although I hadn't been back home from the war for more than a month, I was still getting used to the Texas heat I'd been gone from for close to four years. "Except for them

1

Comancheros, Pa didn't say he'd had much truck with the Comanche of late."

Wash eyed me with a squint, careful like. "What you thinking, Chance?" I'd spent a good deal of our youth getting him in trouble, which had left him a mite gun-shy of me. I could tell by his look that he hadn't forgotten that one troublesome part of me. "I don't like the look on your face."

I had to grin. "Fighting for a losing outfit like them Confederates has made you too cautious, Wash."

"I suppose fighting for the Union has given you all sorts of confidence, huh?"

I grinned at him, knowing I had the upper hand, before urging my horse on toward the cloud of dust, which was slowly getting nearer. What had Wash worried was my curiosity. It had kept my little brother and me in constant trouble in our earlier years. Now, though, I was thirty-two and that was half a lifetime out on this frontier. I was more cautious. Yes sir.

It was hard telling what that mysterious cloud of dust was. Why, it could be anything from a herd of buffalo to some industrious rancher gathering up mavericks to send to market, like some were doing. One thing I knew it wasn't and that was the Comanche that Wash was so worried about. This was their land and they'd been on it a hell of a long time before we'd come along and tried settling on the range. You learn certain things about surviving in this land if you want to stay, and there isn't a better one to learn from than the fellow who was here before you. That's why I knew it couldn't be Comanche, 'cause they wouldn't be so clumsy as to raise that much dust and attention. The only time you'd see that much dust from a

Comanche was when he was riding at you hell-for-leather and meaning for you to die, and believe me, friend, about that time you're going to be more worried about saving your scalp than you are all that dust in the air or where it came from.

"You fought in the western part of the war, didn't you, Wash?" I asked as we slowly walked our horses toward the ever-widening bowl of dust.

"That's a fact, Chance."

"You ever seen anything like this before?" I asked, knowing the war hadn't been over that long for him either.

Wash scratched his head in thought, then his eyes lit up and he pulled up alongside me, a look of urgency about him.

"I'll say! One of them damn Yankee movements heading toward us! Had cannon and supply trains and all that. Why, they'd take their good old time heading right at you, big as life! You thinking that's what we come on?"

I shrugged, my grin now gone. I'd been doing some thinking too. "Makes a body wonder." Without another word I reached back and pulled out my second Colt's Army Model .44 and stuck it in my waistband. Whoever it was making all that dust, they damn sure had us outnumbered. After that thought crossed my mind, I also made a resolution to do something about this curiosity of mine before it got me killed. Wash had taken to carrying a brand new Colt's Navy in his saddlebag as a second gun to the Dance Brothers Model he carried at his side, after our recent run-in with a nasty bunch of Comancheros. But that's a whole 'nother canyon.

3

"Well, I'll be damned," Wash said in amazement as the group came into sight.

"Most of us are, brother, most of us are," was all I replied. It was the guidon and the flag that had caught Wash's eye, but then, I reckon it would, for he had fought for the Confederacy and that's what we were seeing now, a tattered Confederate flag.

Me, I took in the sight of the others before I started looking for a leader. I undid the leather thong I had fashioned on my handmade holster, but even as I did I knew it was useless if a shoot-out was what we were headed into. Hell, there was a good two or three hundred on horseback and God knew how many more walking alongside them.

Except for the rattle of an occasional saber, which was about all the romance any veteran of the War Between the States could stand anymore, I reckon they were a quiet bunch as they pulled up to the banks of the Rio Grande and came to a halt.

Still, I knew that if we started a foofaraw with these fellows, it would be our last. Some carried what looked like those fancy British rifles, Enfields they were called. But the majority of them were loaded for bear, no doubt about it. They sported Sharp's breech-loading carbines in the crook of their arms, and upwards of four—you heard it right the first time—navy revolvers of various sorts. I'd been shot up fighting those Comancheros and my left arm didn't function as well as it should yet, but my eyes still had perfect vision so I knew I wasn't seeing things when I counted derringers, horse pistols, and even a couple of tired old blunderbusses amongst the extra weaponry these lads were carrying.

"Looks like you come a-hunting," I said in as friendly a manner as I could, trying to forget that these very men might well have been on the opposite side of some rifle fire I'd received sometime during the war. Pa once said that forgiving wasn't the easiest chore a man ever had to do, and I was purely about to agree with him right now.

My words went unheeded as the man leading the bunch looked past me and squinted some. I glanced over my shoulder as he said, "Wash? Wash Carston? Is that it? That you, boy?"

Even sitting in a saddle, Wash cut the man a right smart salute.

"Yes, sir." He smiled. "How you be, General?"

The general smiled in friendship as he dismounted. Wash and I dismounted too. "Fine, Wash, just fine," the man said, walking past me and taking ahold of my brother's hand as though he were talking to some long lost soul.

The general my brother knew from somewhere stood tall and erect, although he was a slight man compared to me. I had a notion that even out of uniform he had a good deal of pride about him that kept his body ramrod straight. He was dressed in a well-kept version of the uniform of a Confederate officer. The men about him, although tired looking, had just as much pride, I gauged. He had what I'd call piercing, inquisitive eyes, and by the look of them, I'd say they'd seen a lot in this man's war. What stood this man apart from the rest was a long and heavy black beard and a rather outrageous black ostrich plume that curled wide above the brim of his soft Confederate cavalry hat.

"Ary that thing's got a good point to it, I'd gauge you never lack for a pen to write with," I said, taking in the ostrich plume with a smile. Then I heard at least half a dozen of those Sharp's rifles go to full cock. It got rid of my smile real fast and sent a shiver down my spine.

"General, this here's my brother, Chance," Wash said in a nervous manner. I think he had suspicioned the same thing I had when he heard those rifles being cocked. The difference was that he didn't want to be the first one to open the ball. Wash was cautious the way I needed to be.

"Jo Shelby, Chance," the man said with a cordial smile. The only thing I had left of what had once been my Union uniform was the blue cavalry hat with the crossed sabers on the face of the crown. Offering his hand took mine away from its perch on the butt of my Colt's, which was likely a wise move, but it was my hat that Jo Shelby was taking in. "I never thought I'd say it to a man in blue, but it's nice to meet you."

"Had the same thought running through my mind as well," I said, taking his firm handshake. Still, I thought the man was sincere in his offerings. I cracked a smile, although I'd have to admit it seemed a mite hard coming. "But if my brother says you're all right, that's fine by me."

"You can put them Sharp's back on half cock, fellas," Wash said to the mounted men who'd noticed my blue cavalry hat right off. "I think they struck a truce."

"Don't you think it's 'bout time we got on with what we come here for, General?" a grizzled old sergeant drawled.

"Certainly," the man said and excused himself for the moment. He sure did seem like a civilized sort, and I said as much to Wash.

"Oh, he is, Chance," my brother assured me. "Why, I've heard him quote Shakespeare without reading from the book."

"Got him a memory and manners to boot, huh?"

A quiet seemed to fall over the group now as General Jo Shelby and his sergeant set about to do what it was they had come to the Rio Grande for.

"This is the Rio Grande, isn't it?" he asked once, glancing over his shoulder at me.

"It sure is, General," I said in a civil tone, for I had a notion this wasn't the time to be joshing about anything. "Two miles upstream is a more shallow crossing, if you want to take care of those of your men afoot."

"Thank you, sir," he said, not bothering to face me as he spoke. But I made little of it, for it was plain to see what was going to take place now.

The guidon had come forth and the men had found a sizable rock along the river, which they brought to General Shelby. Silently, ever so carefully, the torn remnants of the Confederate flag were removed from its staff and wrapped around the rock. Once this was accomplished, Shelby took the flag and walked out a few feet into the water. He seemed to be looking for a deep enough place, and as he did his entire troop of men came to attention and gave one final salute. Wash came to attention and did the same. Me, I was likely the last one in the group that did, but I came to attention and saluted the flag too. No one's hand came down until the flag had disappeared from view, forever gone from the sight of these men who had believed in all it meant for nearly six years. It was a strange sort of funeral, but not one any of these men would soon forget.

No one said a word. No one had to. The Confederacy was gone forever now, all except in the hearts and minds of these men. All they had left now were memories of the glorious days they would describe to their grandchildren twenty years from now. And, as always, their grandchildren would think they were heroes of sorts, and in all likelihood they were. But at this moment, I was willing to bet a dollar that each and every one of them felt as though this would be the worst day of their lives, bar none.

"What did you salute for?" one man asked me, an irreverent look about him.

"Just 'cause my flag's still flying don't mean I don't have any respect for yours," I said. "Seems to me a lot of good men died on both sides of that war."

Out of the side of his mouth, Wash whispered, "That may be the smartest thing you've said all day." I have a feeling both of us knew it was.

CHAPTER

★ 2 ★

They had wagons and pack mules filled with supplies, so they weren't starving. Nine twenty-five-mule wagons were filled with everything from whiskey to salt pork and preserves to ammunition. Lots of ammunition.

It would soon be late in the day, so Shelby and his men decided to pitch camp along the Rio Grande and spend one last night before crossing into Mexico, which was where they were headed.

Shelby, it seemed, had never surrendered to a Union general. Nor had he laid down his flag, even though hostilities had officially come to an end. He may have been the only Confederate general to not have really laid down his arms, and his men seemed to be quite proud of that.

Being invited to share some of his salt pork and bacon was an invite I didn't turn down, for we'd been getting tired of prairie chicken for the better part of a week now. Shelby, I found out, was just as pleased to share our coffee.

"Whereabouts you headed down Mexico way, General?" I asked after we finished our meal.

Jo Shelby was about as cautious as a lot of men who had left the war and still hadn't gotten the taste of it out of their mouths. But then, that was to be expected. He gazed at my blue cavalry hat a mite while scratching his beard before giving me an answer.

"Oh, well, I suppose telling you couldn't really hurt us. You've heard of Maximilian, the emperor of Mexico?"

"I've heard of him, although it's my understanding that he's having a mite of trouble keeping that emperor of Mexico title," I said. "Got his own civil war, I hear."

"You're just looking for one more war to fight, that it, General?" Wash asked. Somehow I knew my brother was just saying it to be saying it, for I'd found out during the evening's repast that he'd been assigned to Shelby during the war. Like I say, me and my brother had only been back from the war for a month or so, and he fighting for the south and me the north, why, we hadn't quite gotten around to discussing that tender a subject yet. But one thing I did know was that when you fight under a man, you don't soon forget him or what he stands for, or the way he fights. I'd learned that from Pa long before the war, when he and Wash and I rode together as Texas Rangers. So I'd a notion that my brother knew far better than I why this Confederate general was headed for Mexico.

"In a manner of speaking, yes," the man conceded. He poured the rest of the coffee in our cups and dropped the subject of Mexico.

"Well, gentlemen, you have me at a disadvantage. You know where I'm going, but I still don't know much about you," he said. "Other than the fact that Wash decided to go home when they called a cease-fire, I don't know much about you at all."

"We got a ranch about forty miles north of here, General," Wash volunteered with a good bit of pride.

"You're a little out of your way then, aren't you?"

"An old devil of a mustang busted into our corral and chased out some mares I was gonna breed," I said. "If you knew anything 'bout breeding stock, mister, you'd be willing to chase that damned horse to hell and gone."

The general laughed. "Yes, I would, Mister Carston."

"I say something funny?" I asked, feeling a mite awkward at the moment. I didn't like my words coming back at me.

"He don't mean nothing, Chance," Wash said with a grin. "It's just that the general, why, he had a couple dozen horses shot out from *under* him during the war. That's a fact."

"You see, Mister Carston, I certainly do have an appreciation for good horseflesh. Are you going to pursue this wild mustang?"

"We tracked him down to the Rio Grande about the time you and your men came on us," I said. "Horse is near as smart as a man."

"How's that?"

"His trail ends right at the river here," Wash said. "Must've taken the river north by west or south by east. That's what me and Chance was gonna do when you fellas showed up. Split up and ride the river both directions for a ways till we picked up his trail again."

"I assume that would be just about impossible now," Shelby said.

"Won't argue that one bit," I said. If Shelby did have between three- and five-hundred men with him, not to mention his pack mules and wagons, why, it would be impossible to pick up a trail anywhere around the river now, the way his men were spread out.

"Perhaps I can make this up to you in some way," Shelby said. It could have been a statement or a question.

"You're welcome to try," I said.

"Sergeant, get Jack Terrence and his three friends for me," the general said, and without a question the sergeant was gone.

"What have you got in mind, General?" Wash asked, as curious as I was.

"It's been a long time, but if I remember correctly, gentlemen, you must have not only horses but men to run a ranch effectively. If the two of you set out after this mustang, and there are only two of you, as you say, then the rest of your entire herd could be gone by the time you return, correct?"

Wash shrugged. "Could be."

12

"I have some men who aren't all that keen on going down into Mexico. The only reason they've stayed with me is out of loyalty. Don't get me wrong, I admire that in a man. But I also know that a man functions most effectively if he's doing what he likes. Wouldn't you agree?"

"True," I said, still a mite suspicious of what he was getting at. I reckon I get closemouthed when I get suspicious.

Before he could say any more, four men appeared before the dying fire. Shelby saw I was squinting at them and tossed another piece of deadwood on the dying embers. The fire rose anew and I could better see the faces of the men. When I did, I got up my own self, likely because one of the men was bigger than the others. Besides, I never did like being looked down on by anyone.

"Jack Terrence," the big man said in a voice that had more gravel than drawl to it. Raspy, it was. He sported a mustache that wasn't taken care of at all and he was unshaven, but his grip was firm as he offered his hand. I found myself taking stock in the cautiousness that my brother had, for there was something about this man that seemed awful familiar. The trouble was I couldn't place it.

The three men surrounding him looked hard-bitten to say the least, but if these men had covered as much ground as they appeared to have, that wouldn't be unusual. Hell, Wash and me hadn't shaved in upwards of a week, so there wouldn't be any women hunting us out for companionship either. Blue eyes or brown, it didn't seem to make much difference, they all looked faded and old, although none of the three could have been any older than me. I reckon you learn a lot about age during a war.

"Garver."

"Handy."

"Quartermain."

They spouted off their names, as though answering to some roll call. None offered a hand in friendship, so I didn't either. I simply nodded my head to them and said, "Gents." Recognition deserves the same in return, if you ask me.

"Gentlemen," Shelby said, and I had the notion he was addressing all of us as he spoke, "I believe we can all help one another out." He went on to explain to Terrence and his companions that Wash and I had a ranch up north and how we'd come to be in this area.

"I know most of the men in my outfit and I can assure you that Jack Terrence and his friends are quite good with horses. I've seen them in action and they know what they are doing."

"That a fact," I said, sizing them up as he spoke.

"I wouldn't doubt it, Chance," Wash said. "Seems to me they got enough bow in them legs to have been born to a saddle."

"Polishin' your pants on saddle leather don't make you a rider, Wash." I was still sizing them up, trying to figure out in my own mind whether or not they'd work out.

"It's all up to you men, but I believe that if you give one another a chance, you'll be able to help one another out," Shelby said. With that he picked up his coffee cup and walked away from the fire, leaving only the six of us.

Wash set his cup down by the fire and rose to his full

height, only a few inches shorter than me. He isn't as husky as I am, but I can guarantee you my brother can hold his own in a fight. I know, for I've fought him my own self, and you can't ask for a better guarantee than th...

"...ing?" Terrence asked in his g...

...even
...n the
...g with
...eaking
...es and

...nd. Ary
...nth in a
...l have to
...e food or
...head and
...ers. I ain't
...see him."
...em asked.
...e second to
know, and tha...s... nodded, to
indicate that I'd spoken my piece.

[handwritten note:]
Pat Cotney
Western
Books
536-7505

"I hear some ranchers in this area are thinking of rounding up cattle to take to market up Missouri way," Terrence said. I could see in his eyes he was testing me to see how I'd handle a man like him. "I hear they're paying a hundred dollars for the drive too."

One thing about these cavalry hats. You never could tell whether a man wearing them had been a general or a corporal. Me, I'd been a sergeant. I figured it was about time these fellows knew it and planted my hands on my hips.

"Well, now, friend, I've been hearing it too," I said. "Gotta admit it sounds inviting. Yes, it does. Of course, if you think you can survive rustlers, bushwhackers, and a hundred miles of Indian attacks going through the Nations, at less than a dollar a day"—I smiled here—"and maybe, just maybe not get paid for your troubles, well, lads, you go right ahead. Far be it from me to stop you." My voice hardened. I reckon it was the sergeant in me coming out. "But hear this. Ary you're gonna do it, then do it now or not at all."

"I don't think I like you, mister," the one called Garver said in a growl. He shifted his weight to one side as he spoke, as though he were getting ready to back up his words.

"I've heard those words before," I said. "But I never did like smart asses, either."

His nostrils flared much like those wild mustangs I'd been dealing with this past month or so, as he took in a chest full of air and swung at me. I grimaced as I blocked his swing with my still healing left, brought my left fist down across his cheek and followed it with a hard right cross that stung his jaw as he fell to the ground with a thud.

Out of the corner of my eye I saw his friends going for their guns, but heard the quick cocking of Wash's when they only had their hands on the butts of the cross draw holsters. For a little brother, Wash comes in handy at times.

"Don't ever bait me like that again, sonny, 'cause I don't take to insults. Fact of the matter is, you just ain't good enough to take me, and I've seen better days."

"They's something else you boys gonna have to learn," Wash said, six-gun still in hand. "My brother does most of the talking on the spread, and being the boss, why, he's got him a couple of rules."

"Do tell," Quartermain said, easing his hand off his pistol.

"That's a fact. Rule number one is *the boss is always right.*"

"What if he's wrong?" Quartermain asked.

"Then rule number two takes effect." Wash was silent for a moment.

"Well, what is it?"

"Rule number two is *when the boss is wrong, rule number one applies.*"

"You people work for me, you're gonna do what I tell you and that's that," I said, straightening my hat. "Take the job or leave it, makes no difference to me. We'll be heading north come daylight."

One by one Garver, Handy, and Quartermain said they'd think it over and let me know in the morning. I was about to go back to my fire when I heard Terrence growl a few words.

"I've killed men, Carston."

I looked at him in the crazy sort of way Pa used to look at me when I was a youngster making outlandish remarks.

"Let me tell you something, son. If that's supposed to scare me, it doesn't. Hell, killing people's why folks go to war." I paused a moment before adding, "It's how you kill 'em that makes a difference." I started to turn away before looking back over my shoulder. "Anybody can back shoot a man."

The rest of the night was quiet, although I suspicion Shelby had paid close attention to what was going on. I reckon that was why he didn't speak of it that next morning. I reckon that was also why he offered Wash and me a good helping of his bacon and an extra sack of supplies as we saddled up to ride.

I didn't say anything about Terrence or his men, for I honestly didn't care whether they came along or not. They were the kind who looked like troublemakers from the start, and those were the kind of men I could do without. It was when Wash and I saddled up that the four of them moved in on us from both sides with their horses. I gave them a hard look but said nothing.

"Ten dollars a month is better than nothing," Handy said, "and right now we got nothing."

"I'd bet a dollar you was a sergeant in the goddamn cavalry," Garver said, rubbing his jaw a mite.

"You'd be right," I replied.

"Long as you don't have no more rules to read me, I'll ride along," Quartermain said.

"I ain't a back-shooter," was all Terrence said.

"Well, now, I'm glad to see we got that all cleared up," Wash said with a smile. "Now, what say we stop burning daylight and get back to that ranch and work some of them horses?"

And that was that.

We made it back to the ranch without incident. Our four new hired hands began to open up on the ride back, got right friendly, they did. Wash assured me along the way that they would work out fine, for they had come with General Shelby's recommendation.

In the back of my mind, I kept telling myself I had to keep an eye on this operation. After all, the ranch we were trying to build up had been burned to the ground not long ago but was still serviceable. Our mother had been killed and we'd gone after the Comancheros who'd done the killing; Pa, Wash, and me. Pa couldn't live there anymore, but Wash and me thought we could make a go of it, so it was ours to keep. It was also all we had.

It took a couple of days to get these lads used to what we needed to get done and how we wanted it done, but they seemed to fall to the chores with a willingness that was unusual, considering the first encounter I'd had with them. But then, I reckon you're allowed a mistake once in a while. It was when I got up that fourth morning that I knew I'd been right after all.

Wash claimed Pa and the whole rest of the town could have heard me, even though they were five miles away, I yelled that loud.

You see, when I got up that morning and pulled on my pants and went to throw some water in my eyes, I discovered that the twenty head of horses in the corral were gone.

It only took a little more looking about to find out that our friendly new hired hands were gone, too!

CHAPTER

★ 3 ★

You lost what!"

Pa wasn't too receptive to the idea of our losing a newly formed herd of twenty horses we'd spent close to a month gathering. After all, these fellows had all but taken them out from under our noses, and that doesn't set well with any man. Especially Pa.

"I thought I taught you boys better than that!" Pa had been marshaling while Wash and I were off to war, and it was plain to see he had gotten right good at laying down the law. You bet. "Trust a couple of strangers out of nowhere with your entire stock. Why, I never heard of such foolishness! Never!" He waved

an arm away as he paced back and forth in his office. I
knew he was mad at us, for we'd been listening to him
for all of ten minutes now and he hadn't even offered
us a cup of coffee. And I could use a cup of coffee, the
morning having been too busy for breakfast yet.

"Hell, Pa, you hired Joshua out of nowhere," Wash
said in weak defiance. When you're wrong Pa will nail
you to the wall and to hell with what you feel. Both of
us had found that out in our youth and it had been a
hard lesson to learn, so we tread our ground carefully.
Hell, for all intents and purposes we were grown men,
but as far as Will Carston was concerned we were still
his boys, and making a bad mistake reflected on him.
But then, I reckon only a father would understand
such a thing.

"That's different," he said. "There's some folks you
can tell about right off the bat." He nodded toward
Joshua, his lone deputy. Joshua turned a mite red in
the cheeks as he accepted the compliment, likely
because it wasn't often that a body got those kinds of
things said about him out here.

To hear Pa tell it, Joshua had wandered in out of
nowhere when the man holding the deputy marshal's
job had taken off in search of his own son during the
war. If you were a religious sort, I reckon you could
say that it was as though Joshua, name and all, had
come along just in time. After all, there was a war on
and what with most of the male population gone off to
fight it, why, the Comanche and any number of other
ugly sorts could have their pick of small towns like
Twin Rifles if they had a mind to. Pa and Joshua had
done a good job of seeing that they didn't even try.

"Why, thank you, Will," Joshua said in a humble way. "I don't recall you ever saying that afore. I really do appreciate it." Tall and a mite on the thin side, Joshua could have fit into Wash's clothes if the need arose. I never did ask, but I'd have guessed him to be somewhere between my age and Pa's. My hair was still black while Pa's had a goodly portion of gray in it and Joshua's was starting to show a touch of gray here and there. Where Pa had a full beard, Joshua tended toward a two- or three-day growth of whiskers before taking his face to a razor. Me, I had so thick a growth of whiskers that even when I shaved it looked like I hadn't. Fact of the matter was, there were times when I wondered if that wasn't why Pa had grown a beard.

"Well, I hope you heard it well, Joshua," Pa said, turning his attention back to the problem at hand, "for you won't likely hear it again for some time." He glanced at the two of us, frowned and silently shook his head, still puzzled as to how our herd of horses could have vanished the way it did.

"Actually, Pa, we took those men on good faith," Wash said.

"Yeah," I added, a frown coming to my brow as I took in my brother's words. "That's right, Pa, some general Wash rode with in the war said these were good men." I was beginning to glare at Wash, as I added, "Tells you something about them Johnny Rebs."

Wash was ready to come at me, but Pa saw him and took a quick step in between us.

"Going at each other's throat ain't gonna solve your problems, children," he said in that denigrating tone

22

he used on us when we'd argue with one another, placing a particular emphasis on that last word, *children*. As youngsters it had served its purpose and gotten our attention. As grown men, it was a mite embarrassing to hear the words and realize that we were still capable of acting like children. But then, I reckon brothers can be that way, no matter what their ages.

"Your brother may not be far wrong, G.W.," Pa said. I'd always called my brother Wash, which was the nickname he'd grown up with, but on occasion it was Pa who would call him by the initials of the man he was formally named after, George Washington. "Sounds to me as though the only one those yahoos were any good for was that general who loaned 'em to you."

"No, it couldn't be, Pa." Wash wasn't having any of it. General Jo Shelby had made quite an impression on him, that was clear, and he was going to stand by him. "I rode too long with Jo Shelby to ever believe otherwise."

"Seems to me it's a mite late to be casting blame, fellas," Joshua said. Like always, he'd waited to see how things developed before throwing in his own ideas. But then, I reckon I would too if I was friendly with the whole family and wanted to stay that way. "I'd be heading for the livery and Miss Margaret's to see if she wouldn't fix up some of that leftover roast beef she served up last night." I could see by the expression on his face that he was reliving the eating of that meal. "Right tasty, it was. 'Tain't nothing better for leftovers either, if you was to ask me."

"Joshua's right," Pa said. "Butting heads ain't getting us nowhere. Joshua—"

"I know, Will, I know," the deputy interrupted. "I'll fix up your horses and some druthers while you boys get your fixin's over to Miss Margaret's." He pulled out a pocket watch, opened it, glanced at it, and shut it, then added, "Ary you're smart, you'll get her to fix you up a late breakfast while you wait."

"Sounds good," I said. "See if you can locate some more of those shells for my Spencer, will you, Joshua?"

"Sure thing." He nodded. "You fellers just be off and I'll have more ammunition than you can tote by the time you get through feeding your faces." The way he was shooing us out the door you'd have thought he was the mothering type, and maybe he was. In the short time I'd been back I hadn't heard too much about his past. But then, he wasn't saying, so I wasn't asking.

Pa was silent on the way to the Ferris House, even if it was only a block down and across the street. Like I say, we've got what you'd call a small town in Twin Rifles. The look on Wash's face asked if I knew what was going through Pa's mind but I only shrugged.

Margaret Ferris was a widow who had her cap set on Pa. She must have been some fifteen years younger than Pa, but the years had been good to her for she was still an attractive woman. The only one who had hair as fiery red as hers was her daughter, Rachel, and I had to admit that I'd taken to giving her a looking over more than once since I'd been back. There just hadn't been an awful lot of time for much more than work since I'd gotten back from the war, so romance would have to wait.

"Morning, boys," Margaret said with a smile that was pure sweetness and told you everything you needed to know about how she had successfully run the town's only boardinghouse all by herself. "Will it be breakfast this morning or is the Carston clan just paying a social call?"

"Both," Pa said as we all took off our hats. "We're all needing a decent meal," he added, and we took seats at the large community table used to feed her tenants and anyone else who cared to set down to her meals. "Whatever you've got will suit us fine."

"You could do us one favor, Miss Margaret," I said as she started to walk back to the kitchen.

"Surely, if I can."

"Joshua couldn't talk enough about your last night's roast beef."

She blushed. "He isn't hard to please," she said with a smile.

"Well, if you've got any left over, I was wondering if you could throw together a few sandwiches for us. We'll be leaving shortly after this meal."

She shook her head in wonderment.

"Did I say something wrong?" I asked, hoping I hadn't hurt her feelings, for I really did like her as a woman.

"Nothing, Chance. It just seems that every time I see the three of you together, why, you're going off somewhere." When none of us replied, she added, "Some day you three will realize that a woman likes to be asked out on a picnic once in a while." These last words were directed at Pa.

EX-RANGERS

"Business before pleasure, Miss Margaret," I said, while Pa only mumbled something to himself.

Margaret Ferris shook her head in discouragement and headed toward the kitchen.

Wash was studying a stranger down at the other end of the table, cocking his head this way and that, the way a body does when he's trying to identify someone and the picture just isn't anywhere to be had in your memory.

"Know him?" I asked.

"Ain't sure, Chance. There was an awful lot of men in Shelby's outfit that came and went the time I was with him. After a while, why, you disremember a lot of faces."

"Know what you mean. After a while you figure your mind'll explode ary you try to remember just one more man in your outfit."

Mustaches and beards had taken on a new popularity amongst the men who served in the war and it seemed like every Johnny-Come-Lately had one or was trying to grow one. Some it took to, while others it didn't. The man at the end of the table wore a mustache like a true Texan, drooping over his upper lip to the point of being unkempt. It's hard telling how tall a man is when he's seated, but I was betting this fellow was long in the leg. From his face I would have said he was a mite younger than me, maybe in his late twenties. It was hard telling out here. Between Indians, outlaws, and Mother Nature and Father Time, why, this land could be hell on a body's features. Next to being in a war, I'd gauge the land aged you more than anything.

26

"I don't suppose either of you circled the ranch before riding hell-for-leather into town," Pa said.

"Fact is I did," I said, "although I found the trail I was looking for heading east by south, pretty much like I figured they would."

"You still think they weren't getting extra mounts for Shelby, Wash?" Pa asked.

"No, sir," he said adamantly. "That just ain't Jo Shelby's way."

"I don't know, Wash," I said, thinking back on our meeting with the Confederates. "Seems to me there was an awful lot of those men walking their way to Mexico." I paused as Rachel poured our coffee and we said thanks. "Ain't known a foot soldier yet who wouldn't grab a horse to do his traveling *and* fighting."

"That may be true, but I still can't picture General Shelby putting his men up to something like this." In a way I could understand my brother's feelings, for I'd known my fair share of men during the war that I'd fight next to any day if and when the occasion arose. You meet some mighty good men during a war. Of course, you meet a good share of the crooked and bad ones as well, and no matter who put them up to it, the men we were going to track were a bad lot, of that I was sure.

Margaret and Rachel served up a whole pile of freshly baked biscuits along with individual plates of ham, eggs, and fried potatoes. I couldn't tell who was standing there with a coffeepot, but she kept filling our cups as soon as we'd taken a good gulp of the steaming liquid. I was thankful for it and said as much when I was through cleaning my plate.

27

"You set a fine table," Pa said to the two of them, when Rachel brought out three flour sacks that had the smell of roast beef to them.

"Which way are you heading?" Rachel asked, a serious tone to her voice. Or maybe a mite of worry would be a better description.

"South, it looks like," I said. I briefly told her about what had happened to our new herd of horses. "Until I find out different, I've got a notion we'll be tracking these yahoos back to Shelby's outfit."

I slapped on my hat and was about to leave when Rachel appeared before me and gave me a quick hug. "You take care of yourself, Chance, you hear?" I could have sworn there was a tear in her eye as she spoke. I smiled and gave her a hug back.

"As long as you keep cooking the way you do, there's no way I'm not gonna take care of myself long enough to make it back for another meal."

She blushed but my words had reassured her and she wished me well. I think Margaret was doing something similar to Pa, although I'd been paying so much attention to Rachel that I couldn't be sure. What I did see over my shoulder was the stranger plunking down a coin on the table and getting ready to go too.

I didn't notice that he was following us back to the marshal's office until we'd already reached it and I heard him step up on the boardwalk behind us.

"Excuse me, gents," he said with a cordial smile. I was wrong, he wasn't long in the leg but was only average in height. "I couldn't help but hear you fellas talking about heading south toward Jo Shelby's out-fit."

"What about it?" I said. I found myself getting suspicious, for the man had been nursing no more than a cup of coffee most of the time we'd been eating our meal. If I wasn't mistaken, Rachel had taken his plate not long after we'd set down. Or maybe a good healthy dose of suspicion was the order of the day for me. I wasn't sure.

"Nothing. I was just wondering if you could use some company on the way. I'm looking for Shelby myself," he said in what sounded like a Texas drawl that made me feel a mite better about the man. "Times being what they are and all"—he shrugged—"I just figured you might be able to use another gun along the way."

"Pa? Wash? What do you think?" I asked. My brother and father reappeared in the doorway and did the same sizing up of the man as I had. He seemed to be built well enough to take care of himself.

"Where you from, mister?" Wash said.

The man smiled. "A lot of places I'd just as soon forget. War does that to a lot of men, I reckon."

I knew what he was talking about. What with the war being over, there would be a lot of men heading west who would just as soon leave their past behind them. *War is a strange business that tends to make heroes and cowards out of normal men.* A man is pressed beyond what he thought his limits were and soon finds out what he can and can't do. It results in a lot of men never going back home because of it, and it's not just being a hero or a coward or anything in between. *Sometimes you just can't go back home because of what the war has done to you.* Shelby and his men were a good example of that. Yes sir, I knew what this man was talking about.

"Would I be knowing you from somewhere?" Pa asked.

"I ain't *that* bad a man, friend." The man smiled again, seeing the badge on Pa's shirt front. Still, I thought I sensed a mite of uneasiness about him at the sight of a lawman's badge. Maybe it was just that I was looking for the bad in everyone now that I'd been set on edge.

"Then you'll do." Pa nodded. "We can always use another storyteller around the campfire," he added with a smile of his own, wanting to make the man feel at ease, I reckon.

I shrugged. "You can leave or stay, I reckon. I'd expect you to pull your own weight as far as providing for a meal now and then." I paused a moment in thought, giving both Pa and this man a scowl before I spoke. "Tell you what, mister, you take care of the hunting on this trip and we'll do the tracking. But that better be all you do, for I ain't a mind of any funny business, not from you or anyone else. Understand?"

"Suits me fine." He stuck out a paw. "Pleased to meet you."

We introduced ourselves, each taking his hand and identifying ourselves.

"Fine. Listen, give me ten minutes and I'll be ready to go. I've got to check on a shotgun over at the gunsmith shop."

"You bet," I said. "Say, what'd you say your name was?"

He paused a moment in thought before saying,

"Ben, just call me Ben." He then started down the street.

I glanced at Pa as we all watched him go.

"I know what you're thinking, Chance," he said, as though reading my mind. "And I agree. Somewhere not too far back, I'd bet a dollar that man's run afoul of the law."

CHAPTER
★ 4 ★

Margaret and Rachel were standing on the porch of the Ferris House when we left, gently if not sadly waving to us as we walked our horses out of town. All of us, including Ben—or whatever his name was— tipped our hats to the ladies as we left town.

"I can see you fellas are coming back," Ben said with a smile. Wash frowned at the man, then remembered that he was present when Margaret and Rachel were paying more than casual attention to Pa and me.

"Oh, yeah. Sure," Wash said.

"Where you going, Wash?" another voice said as we neared the southern edge of town. The voice belonged to Sarah Ann Porter, the girl who was turning into a

32

woman with each passing day, especially as far as Wash was concerned. I reckon the three of us Carstons had at least gotten lucky in the woman category of life when the war was over. Having someone care about you always makes it easier coming back, not to mention giving you incentive to come back. Sarah Ann was Wash's incentive.

"Manhunting, Sarah," Wash said as we continued to ride on. "You talk to Rachel and Margaret. They'll tell you," he added over his shoulder as we reached the edge of town.

"Yes, sir," Ben said with a smile as he took in Sarah Ann's fiery red hair and beautiful body, "I can see you boys are definitely coming back."

It was still early in the morning so we gave the horses a workout as we headed south by east toward what I knew would be the same tracks I had encountered outside the ranch. Sure enough, they were bigger than life, right where I suspected they would be. Hell, a blind man could have followed the trail. But then, following a trail of twenty horses wasn't going to be the hardest part of our job.

We followed them at a steady pace for the better part of twenty miles south, heading almost in the same direction as Wash and I had trailed the first horses we had lost. It was some past noon when we stopped at a water hole and gave the horses a rest.

"We keep heading in this direction, I'm gonna have more and more doubts about your good general, Wash," I said as I loosened the cinch on my saddle and let my mount drink his fill.

"I know how it looks, Chance, but you'll have to have more than just suspicions to prove otherwise to me," Wash replied. After a bit of silence and a drink of water, he added, "Reminds me of the first time we chased that mustang." Wiping an arm across his brow, he said, "Sure does seem like hard work."

Pa chuckled. "I don't know how it could be hard work for you, son, when it's your horse that's been doing it all," he said.

Ben smiled at the comments but said little. So far he had been pretty tight-lipped, but I wasn't going to press him. If he wanted to talk, I figured he'd do so in time. Until then, there were better things to be done than palaver over a body's past.

We gave the horses a good rest, eating jerked beef with water in the meantime. There was no question about whether we'd have coffee or not. Hell, it was almost an unwritten rule that, as precious as it could be, you saved it for a meal that was worth drinking it with. Coffee would be had at supper with some of the Ferris women's roast beef sandwiches. Besides, coffee had gotten a whole lot more drinkable since those Arbuckle boys had taken to roasting the beans. Yes sir.

"Gents," I said, tightening the cinch on my horse as we readied to ride again, "I'd suggest we take it easy this afternoon and give these horses their heads. 'Tain't gonna get any cooler till evening and these are the only mounts we've got."

"Makes sense," Pa agreed, mounting up. "Only thing that's gonna get rid of these tracks is a good norther, and I ain't looking for one any time soon, ary my bones be correct."

With full canteens we headed south again, spread out in an even line this time, since the horses had apparently gotten a mite out of control at the water hole. The yahoos we were following had had to round up some of the horses who had taken to running wild after having their fill of water, or so it seemed from the tracks. Like I figured, the trail narrowed some as we got a mile or two down the road and the riders had more control of the herd.

It got hot that afternoon and I was glad I had that kerchief on my neck. We didn't do much palavering for there was little to talk about. The routine got to be me, Pa, and Wash doing the tracking while Ben rode behind us and kept an eye out for game for the evening fire and anything else that might be in the area that needed noticing. Like the Comanche.

It took twice as much time to cover the amount of ground we had that morning, but we were persistent about it and reached the Rio Grande not far from where we'd run into Shelby and his Confederate force close to sundown.

"One stringy jackrabbit is about all I conjured up today, boys," Ben said in a shy manner. "I confess, I've seen better hunting country."

"Long as we got a fire to do for us we'll make a go of it," I said, not complaining. You didn't have to be a veteran of any war to appreciate having food at the end of the day, for nearly every man had gone without at one time or another and had no cause to complain.

Wash and me took care of the horses while Pa got a fire going and began boiling some coffee, and Ben skinned his rabbit.

"Quiet sort, ain't he?" Wash said, working on his saddle and gear.

"Long as he don't throw down on me, he can be as quiet as he likes," I said. To myself, I added in a

35

mumble, "And I do believe he could throw down on a body if he'd a mind to."

We ate what we could off that jackrabbit. It wasn't much for four men, mind you, but it was warm food and to a body's stomach that's what matters at the end of the day. When we'd picked that rabbit clean, I broke out some of Margaret's roast beef sandwiches and rationed a half of one to each of us. There was still a bit of sun left to set by the time we'd finished eating, so I decided to make use of it.

"We come on some tumbleweed today, as I recall," I said, swallowing the last of my coffee. "Reckon I'll check the horses and see if they've got any stickers in their legs."

"I'll join you," Ben said. "Man not taking care of his horse ain't much more than lazy in this land."

I nodded agreement.

"I'll round up some more firewood," Wash said. "You want to help me, Pa?"

Pa just smiled and shook his head. "Age before beauty, son. You go right ahead."

"What're you gonna do?"

An amazed look came to Pa's face. "Why, guard the coffeepot, of course!" One thing about Pa, he hadn't lost his sense of humor.

It's a good thing Ben and I took to checking the horses, for two of them had, indeed, picked up some of the stickers from the tumbleweed. We set to fixing them up with what little light we had left.

"Did your riding for the Union, did you?" Ben said, all of a sudden yearning for talk. Or maybe he just liked to do his talking from one man to another. Some men are like that. They shy away from crowds for one reason or another.

"That's a fact," I said, still working on my mount's leg. "You?"

"Started out with Rip Ford's boys."

"Good men," I said. "Fought the last battle of that goddamn war, from what Wash tells me."

"So they say."

"Didn't spend the whole war with Rip?" I asked after a silence that seemed rather heavy between the two of us.

"Nope. Second Texas Cavalry and a few others," Ben said. After another lengthy pause, he added, "Got transferred around some."

Mind you now, neither one of us had been doing anything more than working on the horses while we palavered. It was when I heard Ben say he'd been transferred around some that I stopped what I was doing and looked over my shoulder and right into Ben's eyes as I said, "I see."

We finished up what we were doing in silence, getting all of the stickers out of the two horses by the time dark had set in. But all the while I knew that Ben was thinking the same thing I was, that he might just have been stretching the blanket some with his exploits of the war.

Transferred some? I'm laughing! The only reason anyone got transferred in that war was because he was a troublemaker or an officer, sometimes the two being the same. But an enlisted man, transferred? Not hardly! You joined a unit and stayed with it throughout the war, until the conflict was over or you died.

Hell, there was always a shortage of troops, even in the Union Army, which outnumbered the Johnny Rebs most of the war. So I knew good and well that the same problem existed in the South with their own troops. Transfer? Not hardly!

"You know, Chance," Ben said after we'd finished and were still out of earshot of Wash and Pa at the fire, "war sure is a hard life for a body."

"Wouldn't argue that one bit." I found myself with mixed emotions about this man, feeling like I could take a liking to him if he'd give me half a chance, yet wondering at the same time if I could trust him, especially after our short conversation about the war. Or maybe it was the fact that being taken in by the yahoos we were trailing had made me a mite more distrustful than usual.

"Body gets a chance to get in more trouble than usual too."

I nodded in silence while the man shyly fumbled for words.

"I just wouldn't want you to get the wrong idea," he said in a low, almost shameful voice. "You know, like I was some kind of deserter."

"Thought never crossed my mind," I said in total honesty with the man, although talk of a deserter now made more sense to me than the prospect of a man being a troublemaker. There had been a lot of desertion on both sides of the war. I knew he damn sure wasn't an officer. I smiled, gave him a friendly slap on the shoulder. "Like you said, Ben, a body can get in an awful lot of trouble in the army. Any army."

A look of relief came to his face now as he half smiled and took great strides back to the fire.

"I hope you fellas left a cup's worth of that coffee," he said. "I mean to tell you it gets mighty cool without that sun out."

I decided then and there to take a chance and play it by ear. I'd try my best to put some trust in this Ben. I also made a pact with myself that if he didn't turn out to be on our side, on my side, well, I'd take care of that right quick too.

I'd kill the son of a bitch!

CHAPTER
★ 5 ★

We each took a two-hour turn at guard that night, but the only noise was the rustle of the water of the river. Pa had the last watch, so it was understandable that the three of us woke up to the smell of coffee brewing an hour or so before daylight. I saw the small fry pan in his big hand before I smelled the bacon frying in it.

"Can't offer much more'n a couple pieces of this stuff each, lads, but you sop up the grease with a biscuit and I've a notion the coffee will do for the rest of the meal," Pa said with a bit of a smile. He must have already had at least one cup of coffee, for I couldn't picture him being cordial about much of anything this early in the morning. But then, I'd been away to war for a few years, and they tell me people change.

"Better put that badge away, Pa," I said when I'd had my own first cup of coffee. It was having some of that Arbuckle's on hand in the morning that made me wonder why they hadn't voted those coffee-roasting brothers to Congress yet. Yes sir, it surely did have a taste to it, that coffee.

"Oh, yeah," Pa said with a squint, still frying up the bacon. "I almost forgot."

"Your piece of tin won't do you much good from here on out."

"That's right," Ben said before Pa could reply. "Once you git across the Rio, why, it's gun law and common sense that'll keep you alive."

"Got a point, lad," Pa mumbled. One thing about Pa, he never did talk too loud if he was admitting to someone else's being right. I reckon some folks are like that. Or maybe it's a body's age. "Must be getting old." He thumbed the marshal's badge on his chest then looked back at the river we'd camped by. "Looks like they got away."

"Not hardly!" I said, feeling my blood boil a lot hotter than the coffeepot on the fire.

"Legally, son, that's a boundary," Pa said, taking in more coffee.

"Like hell!" I said through gritted teeth. "That ain't nothing but a goddamn stream! I'll follow those yahoos to hell if that's what it takes to get those horses back!"

It was still dark when we finished eating, in what can only be described as a tense silence. But the sun wasn't far from coming over the horizon, so we broke camp quickly and readied our horses for the day. Hell, it might have been before sunup but I wasn't going to burn any more daylight than possible if it could be helped. Especially what with the afternoon heat being what it was. It was best to be up and ready to track once the first inkling of sun was upon us.

Without a word I saddled up and headed across the river.

"Where you going?" Wash asked, dumbfounded.

I reined in my horse midstream and looked over my shoulder. "I didn't ride forty miles to be stopped by a so-called boundary, little brother. Hell, you oughtta know better. The damned horses are yours as much as mine." By the time I was on the far side of the Rio Grande, Wash was by my side.

I looked over my shoulder and Pa was mounting up and then Ben. The scowl on his face became clearer and clearer as he crossed the river and pulled up beside me.

"I reckon someone's got to go along to keep you children in line," he grumbled, not all that enthused about the idea of invading Mexico.

"What about you, Ben?" I asked.

"Well, gents, it has been my experience that there is only one thing worse than riding with a family that continually argues amongst themselves," he said, a hint of a smile about him.

"And what's that?"

"Riding alone." He paused a moment, taking in the country that was becoming more and more desertlike as we rode south. "And I'll tell you something, gents, I ain't riding this country alone. No sir."

We spread out wider than we had the previous day.

Once again the horses had gotten out of control some when they had crossed the Rio and it took a bit of doing to get them back into some kind of formation, so we took the first quarter mile or so real slow.

I don't know about the rest of the group, but once we got across the river I had a case of the shivers, and it wasn't from the early morning coolness. I reckon it was the conscious knowledge that I was now in Mexico and entering a country that was just as much at war as the North and South had once been.

It wasn't that I hadn't been in Mexico before, for I had, as a Texas Ranger with Pa and Wash before the war. Back then they were still arguing about whether or not the Rio Grande was the southern border of Texas, so we didn't pay any attention to the river when it came to chasing down Indians or bandidos. We just took off after them until we got them and brought them back to Texas, one way or another, if you know what I mean. I reckon that was also why I'd gotten a mite disturbed at Pa's remark about the yahoos we were trailing getting away. There are some things you learn that become force of habit, like tracking down your man until you get him, whether you have to go to hell and back to do it or simply across the street. All three of us had picked that up as rangers before the war. For me and Wash, I reckon old habits die hard. I found myself having my doubts about Pa though. Maybe working in a civilized city and not being an active ranger for upwards of five years had softened him. It was something to think about.

I knew that normally Mexico was a land where you had to watch out for the land itself more than the people in it. The people of this land were a peaceful sort who wanted nothing more than to mind their own business. But they were now embroiled in a war between Benito Juarez and a self-proclaimed emperor by the name of Maximilian, the man Shelby and his volunteers were on their way to help out. I reckon it was that knowledge that gave me the shivers as I crossed the Rio Grande. I had no idea how far Shelby and his men had gotten, but I did recall hearing that Juarez had some of his men patrolling the Rio Grande border. I also knew that Juarez had the people of Mexico stirred up about this Maximilian fellow and that they were taking this revolution or civil war seriously. It didn't make me feel any easier about crossing into Mexico to look for my stolen horses.

"Looking a mite bothered, son," Pa said when the sun had brought first light and he could see the expression on my face.

"You could say that."

"What's bothering you?"

I half smiled. "Just remembering something you told me years ago."

"And just what piece of wisdom was that?"

"We'd crossed the Rio looking for some other horse thieves, as I recall, and you told me and Wash to keep an eye out for the rurales."

"Sounds like my words," Pa said, not quite sure what I was getting at.

"You also said something to the effect that Mexicans had no love of Americanos. Couldn't stand to have Americanos come to save 'em from anyone, 'cause then they'd have a hell of a problem figuring out how to get us *out* of their country."

44

Pa smiled, remembering the words. "It was true then and likely even truer now," he confirmed.

"I wonder if them fellers figure us for a problem?" Ben said, nodding his head toward the east.

"I reckon we'll find out soon enough," Wash said, unhooking the thong on his Dance Brothers revolver as he spoke.

"You take it easy on the fireworks, son," Pa said, seeing the same thing I did and knowing that talking was likely more appropriate an action at the moment.

There were at least a dozen, maybe fifteen, riders wearing wide sombreros and armed to the teeth with six-guns and knives, and an occasional rifle riding our way. I reckon Ben had indeed been in the cavalry during the war, for he didn't need to be told to spread out as the force of men neared us. That put Wash out on one side and Ben out on the other, while me and Pa faced the men.

"How do, amigos," Pa said when the time seemed right. Of course, you never could tell what was the "right" time for anything with cutthroats like these. At least, that's how they impressed me. As for amigos, well, hoss, I wouldn't have asked any of them to squat for coffee even if I had it to dish out. I didn't like them and it showed and I didn't care.

Pa glanced at me, glared and said, "You'll have to forgive Chance here. He's a real fire-eater and we had a cold breakfast." Wash and Ben smiled. So did one of the men who looked like he might be mean enough to handle this bunch of toughs.

The leader began spouting off in Mexican, pounding a fist on his chest and rattling off a half-dozen names that likely took him back to his grandfather's ancestry. I figured him for a long-winded sort.

"That's fine, Jefe, just fine," Pa said, "but I ain't palavering in your lingo today. Besides, I saw you smile, so I know you can talk a mite of Anglo ary you've a mind to."

Jefe, or whatever his name was, frowned at Pa, thinking hard about what he should do next. He could fish or cut bait, and likely do us all in during the process if he wanted. I reckon that was why I made sure he saw me unhook the thong of my own Colt's real slow and deliberate like. Right along with it I gave him a hard look that said he was going to be the first one to die if anyone pulled a gun in his outfit. I had a notion it made him think twice. Or maybe he was just getting up the mad to take on all four of us by his lonesome.

"I must know what you are doing here, senors," he said after what appeared to be a long silence.

"I'd tell you minding my own business," I half growled, "but I doubt you'd believe me." It crossed my mind, from the look on Pa's face, that he was hoping they were going to ignore my remark.

"We come a-looking for some horses some bad hombres stole from our ranch," Pa said. "Four men, twenty horses. I don't suppose you gents seen 'em, have you?"

"They're Anglos, Mister Jefe, just like us," Wash said when the other man failed to answer. "We're just trying to get rid of the bad men in the country, same as you." When that didn't stir any emotion or comment amongst the group, he added, "You *are* riding for El Presidente Juarez, ain't you?"

"Juarez? *Si!* Of course!" Jefe said with a great deal of pride, although I had an idea it was false at best.

For a little brother, Wash was catching on right quick. He'd drawn on the man's pride and given him an excuse for being out here as well when he associated this bunch with Juarez. More than likely they were the cutthroats I had first imagined, but if associating them with the current civil war and the hero of the country would put us in good with them, then I was all for it, yes sir.

"But we have not seen these bandidos you speak of." He paused a moment in thought. Hell, they hadn't seen the yahoos we were after because these toughs had just come into the area too. If they were riding for Juarez, I'd eat my hat! "We must check the Americanos who come into our country now. Many come to fight in our war and, being with Juarez, we must know where their loyalties lie." He scratched his unshaven jaw, cocked an eye at me and said, "Tell me, senor, where do *your* loyalties lie?"

I yanked a thumb over my shoulder. "When I get right back across the border, my loyalties are on Yankee soil," I said. "But seeing the way you people take to treating foreigners, why, I reckon my loyalty lies with Mister Colt," I added, running my hand along the holster, just to let him know I was ready to open the ball if he had a mind to dance.

Pa was all of a sudden throwing hard glances at me and I reckon you couldn't blame him. Here I was fixing to go to war while he was doing his damnedest to keep the peace. I'd hear about it, of that I was sure.

"Look, Jefe," Pa said, "you've got business and we've got business. Believe me, I wish your Senor

Juarez all the luck in the world. But we ain't doing nothing but burning daylight, what with all this palavering we're doing. Now, I suggest that you go back to patrolling these borderlands, while we catch up with these *gringos* who stole our horses and get out of your way." Pa smiled quick, the way one of those politicians does when he's looking for a fast handshake and a promise of a vote.

"I do not know, senor," Jefe said with a mite of hesitation. I do believe he would have given the signal for his men to open fire if he'd had time to think about it all. But while Pa and me were wondering what to do, Ben, who'd been silent so far, took a hand and made up the man's mind right quick.

"I wouldn't spend an awful lot of time thinking about that invite, mister," Ben said. I heard the cocking of his pistol in the silence before I heard his words or saw the expression on his face. But once I saw it I knew he meant business. The Remington in his fist was resting right on top of his saddle horn, pointing at Jefe and the man on either side of him. But the words were aimed at this so-called fearless leader, and I don't think he liked the situation he was being put in.

Jefe began cussing something fierce in his own language, aiming the words at his cohorts as they spewed from him.

"I don't think he likes you," I said, feeling a smile come to my face.

"I know what he said," was Ben's hard reply. "He don't git his sorry ass outta here, I'm gonna make buzzard bait outta him and a few of his compadres

48

real quick." With those last words he cocked an eye at Jefe, as though that made him look more evil. Or maybe he was trying to make them believe he had a glass eye. Hell, I don't know. But it worked.

All of a sudden Jefe got red in the face, even for a man as darkly tanned as he was, wheeled his mount in an about-face and led his men back in the direction they had come from.

I think all of us breathed a sigh of relief. I know I did.

"I was beginning to wonder how long you'd keep silent," Pa said with gratitude. "I'm obliged to you for taking a hand."

"Yeah, especially when you didn't have to," I added. "Wasn't your fight." It gave me a better feeling about him than I'd had so far.

Ben shrugged and smiled. It was the kind of smile that said he was enjoying the whole thing. For a second it bothered me, then I remembered how he'd helped us out in a pinch.

"Well, boys, it's like this," he said. "I always make it a rule to let the other fellow fire first. If a man wants to fight, I argue the question with him and try to show him how foolish it would be. If he can't be dissuaded, why, then the fun begins, but I always let him have first crack. Then when I fire, you see, I have the verdict of self-defense on my side. I know that he is pretty certain, in his hurry, to miss.

"I never do." He said this last with the cocky smile of a man who is certain of himself, and I do believe he was.

I recall Pa telling us in our youth that first, there was

the way a man saw himself. Second, there was the way others saw a man. And last, there was the way a man really was. Pa said the odds of all three of those visions being the same were close to impossible.

"Anything you say, hoss," I said before we got back to tracking those horses.

It was at noon camp that Pa let me know his thoughts on the fracas we'd nearly gotten into earlier in the morning.

"You remember me telling you back in your youth that having a big mouth never made a big man?" he asked as he took a pull on his canteen and bit off a piece of jerked beef like it was nothing. The yank gave a twisted look to his face, and the anger in his voice only intensified the situation.

"That I do, Pa," I said. Pa had taught us to take our licks when we were wrong and to stand our ground when we were right. I could do both, but when it came to me and Pa hassling over something, why, it was usually one of us thinking the other was wrong while we were right. But then, butting heads is usually like that, I reckon.

"Well, you want to keep that in mind the next time you try picking a fight with a band of toughs that outnumber you as much as those Mexican lads did this morning." The words came out as harsh as I'd ever heard them. "I may be getting old, but I've got a few good years left in me, and by God, I'd like to live long enough to enjoy 'em!" He nodded, then added, "Keeping you out of the grave isn't something I relish for a full-time job, you know."

"I didn't tell you to come along, Pa," I said in my own harsh manner. "You get the itch, you just hightail it back to Twin Rifles. The law's no good here anyway."

I do believe that any more palavering or arguing and me and Pa would have gone heel and toe. Wash had the good sense to stay out of it, having been whipped by both Pa and me at one time or another. It was Ben who stepped in before we could go any further.

"I was you, Chance, I'd thank my lucky stars your Pa did come along. Why, if he didn't, they'd have been using you for target practice by now," he said. "Of course, it wasn't the law that had anything to do with why Will come along."

These last words sort of caught me and Pa off guard, so Ben continued.

"Why, he come along 'cause you're family," Ben said. "And everybody knows that when you come right down to it, why, family is all you've got in this world."

It sounded so simple and made so much sense that Pa and me just grumbled at one another and shut up for a while.

"Tell me something, Ben," Wash said later. "How is it you figure riding alone is worse than riding with a family who argues, like you said this morning?"

"Well, Wash, it's like this," Ben said. "Riding with the likes of you folks, why, all there is to do is listen to the three of you yammer back and forth. Why, I'd never get a word in edgewise."

"I see." It sounded simple enough. "How's that better than riding alone?"

"Why, if I was to ride alone, I'd have no one to listen to me but me, and I'm so boring a talker that I'd likely put myself to sleep before high noon!" Ben got a

51

laugh out of all three of us and eased the tension in camp by doing so. Me, I didn't figure him for a boring man at all.

The day had nearly the same pattern we'd followed the previous day, getting as much riding done as possible during the morning hours and taking it easy during the afternoon when we gave the horses a rest. We covered a fair amount of ground and it looked like we were gaining on those yahoos, but my eyes surely did get tired by the end of the day.

I had to rub my eyes when I thought I saw an outrider of sorts on the horizon. When I looked a second time, he was gone.

CHAPTER

★ 6 ★

Rattlesnake was the main course for supper that night. They are a gruesome reptile to be sure, but once you get past the fact that you're eating it, why, rattlesnake is right tasty. I reckon with a bit of imagination you can convince yourself that you're eating chicken if you're that skittish about the whole thing. I recall Wash, as a child, being convinced that the chicken he was eating was fish because the white meat of one looked the same as the other. That was when I found out how much the power of suggestion was worth.

We had been silent most of the day, concentrating on tracking down the horse thieves. We'd stopped only late in the afternoon, when we'd come on a water hole that looked suitable.

"Turned out to be pretty handy with that six-gun of yours," Pa said to Ben after supper.

"Well now, Will, I've been finding out more and more out here that it does indeed pay to be handy with a weapon," Ben said, a trace of a smile cracking the corner of his mouth.

When Ben said no more, I followed Pa's suit and made a comment aimed at opening him up some.

"Handle that Remington like you've been in a tight spot more than once, Ben."

He smiled briefly and shrugged. "Man's got to be good at something, I reckon." He paused then, the smile suddenly gone as his eyes began to shift from Pa to me to Wash and back. "You fellas are awful curious all of a sudden."

This time I was the one who shrugged. "Just saying my say."

He took us in again, just like the first time, sizing each of us up like so much beef on the hoof. It didn't take much to see that he was mulling over something mighty strong in his mind. And I'd a notion that we were about to become part of it.

"All right, fellas, I'll satisfy your curiosity," he said. That hint of a smile came to the corner of his mouth again and he added, "Besides, you can't arrest me. We're in Mexico, right?"

"True enough," Wash said, pouring the rest of the coffee. Pa was silent about the comment, but I figured he had his own thoughts on that.

"You're right, Will, I'm fairly good with this gun. Of course, I've been in my share of fandangos too. Went

54

back to Austin, where my wife lives, after the war and got involved in a shooting with some occupation troops. Damn fool bastards," he muttered.

I saw the fire light up in Pa's and Wash's eyes as Ben said the words *occupation troops*. Me, I remembered the trouble we'd had not long ago with the so-called occupation troops and the way we'd handled it, but I also found myself a mite suspicious of the man telling the story. I figured I'd wait until the rest of the story was out before I got excited about anything.

"I didn't kill any of them," Ben said, "although I often wished I had." He didn't embellish the circumstances, but simply said, "They put me in jail, but I bribed the guards and escaped. I'd heard about this Maximilian fellow and some of the other rebels heading down Mexico way, so I came to the conclusion that crossing the border might not be such a bad idea, being a wanted man and all."

"I know how you feel about them occupation troops," Pa said and began telling our new riding companion about the trouble we'd had in Twin Rifles not long ago.

"I'm gonna check those horses," I said and left the area. Hell, I'd been a part of it all so there wasn't anything about the story that I didn't already know.

"I'll join you," Wash said. It made sense, for he was there too.

The horses were in better shape than they had been the night before and required little attention as far as pulling stickers out of their legs.

"What do you think of that?" Wash said, digging around in his saddlebags until he came up with a pistol that was definitely not a Colt nor a Remington.

That was Wash, still showing off when he had a new toy. I studied it in the last minutes of light.

"Where the hell'd you get that?"

"At Kelly's Hardware. Some fella brought it in and traded it off for another handgun. It's a LeMat."

"Whatever you say, brother." He handed me the gun and I studied it further. Wash filled me in as I gandered at this odd-looking duck.

The LeMat was apparently one of the Confederate's more popular foreign built handguns during the war. Its inventor was an American-born Frenchman. A few years before the war, in New Orleans, he had fashioned a percussion weapon with what looked like two barrels, one on top of the other. And that's what it was. It was just that the arbor pin, around which the cylinder revolved, was in the form of a second large barrel. At first, I couldn't figure out what that second barrel could be, but Wash was only too eager to explain.

"It's got two surprises, Chance," he said with pride.

"What's that?"

"It's only a .40 caliber, but it fires *nine* shots."

"Impressive if you like the odd shape." I couldn't see how anyone could hold onto the handle, for it had no curve to it, as though it weren't made to fit in a hand at all.

"See this?" Wash ran his finger along the bottom barrel, if that's what it was, then slowly turned it in my direction so I could see the gaping end of it in the fading light of day.

"What the hell—"

"It's a shotgun." Wash nodded with pride. "You flip this little switch and it fires a shotgun round. It—"

A frown came to me as I quickly put a finger to my lips and perked my ears right up. I was hearing something other than the voices of Ben and Pa by the campfire. It was the far side of camp and it sounded like a new saddle creaking as someone dismounted slowly.

"I knew I wasn't going blind," I said in a low mumble, remembering the outrider I thought I'd seen as we made camp at the water hole. When Wash threw me a curious look, I whispered, "It's them goddamn Mexicans we met up with this morning."

No sooner was I through with the sentence than Wash's Dance Brothers .44 was out of its holster and he had two six-guns in his fists. Me, I pulled the bowie knife from my left side as I palmed my Colt's Army Model .44. I was one of those men who liked to carry a second gun in his saddlebags, but right now I didn't have time to get it, and if I did try I might spook the horses. I knew I could make due with what I had in hand. Besides, I had a notion Wash was going to be eager to show off that LeMat pistol he'd just showed me, so there would be plenty of fireworks on his part.

"Move around to the left and make believers out of these bastards, but don't go firing across the camp," I said.

Wash frowned. "How come?"

"I'm gonna be on the other side." Sometimes I wondered about my little brother.

I hadn't moved ten feet around to the right before I heard a couple of men break into camp, guns drawn. It was then I remembered there were a good dozen of those toughs and a dose of panic crossed my mind as I realized one six-gun wasn't going to be enough. I'd need more. Seeing Jefe with his guns drawn and aimed at Pa's guts drove home the point. I'd simply have to *take* another gun.

The sun had gone down and we were far enough out so that the cactus could hide us momentarily. Ben and Pa had been so engrossed in their storytelling that they'd forgotten to put any more wood on the fire, so that helped our situation too.

I was trying to keep an eye out for the cutthroats I knew would come my way and see what Jefe would try with Pa.

"You didn't think I would let you leave the country without paying for such an insult, did you, senor?" Jefe snarled. It was then that I realized he wasn't spouting off to Pa. It was Ben he was planning on killing. Ben had showed him up for the coward he was and no man likes that. The damn fool was so full of killing Ben that he'd clean forgotten to ask where Wash and me were. He cocked his pistol and I stepped out in the open, barely visible in the darkness.

"Jefe!" I yelled and pulled the trigger the same time he was raising his gun to me. The bullet went right through his head and he was dead long before he hit the ground.

Pa grabbed the gun from his lifeless hand and pulled out his own Remington. Soon Ben and Pa were back-to-back, potshotting any takers who wanted to die before the sun rose again.

I shot two more who rushed around the side at me, one of them grazing my side before he died. On the far side of camp I could hear Wash's LeMat firing as quick as he could pull the trigger. Subconsciously, I counted to six, then heard him stop for a split second.

"Get him!" a deep Mexican accent yelled and I could see in my mind how it would be. However many there were would rush my brother and he would kill three of them with his surprise three extra shots. I was right. But I'd forgotten about the shotgun blast that filled the air. A cry went out, the kind of cry that is let out by men who have caught a fair amount of buckshot in them, enough to make them live to tell about it. Then the gunfire subsided.

I rushed across the camp, only a step or two behind Pa and Ben. I stopped only once, to see about four of the remaining crowd of would-be killers mounting up and hightailing it out of there as fast as their horses could carry them. The bodies of four dead Mexicans lay on Wash's side of the camp.

"What the hell was that?" Pa said, bursting past the cactus and giving his youngest son a look over.

"His surprise," I said, with what must have been a lopsided grin.

"Yeah," Wash said in the same manner, then proceeded to show Pa his new toy and how well it worked.

Ben took me by the elbow and steered me back to the fire where we got it going full strength again. I had a notion these yahoos weren't going to be back.

"You saved my life, Chance," Ben said. I could tell he was grateful about the whole thing. "I'm obliged."

"That'll make us even."

"You know, you're a good man in a tight spot," he said when Pa and Wash came back to the fire.

"Like I said, that makes us even."

And I reckon it did.

CHAPTER
★ 7 ★

I think all of us slept kind of light that night, just in case any of Jefe's band of varmints decided to return and make a heroic stand of some sort to avenge their fallen leader. I knew that if I was asked, I'd admit to it without any pangs of guilt. Hell, I'd wanted to stay alive. But the only real bothersome thing that night was the cold night air. Compared to the heat we faced all afternoon, the quick cooling off after sunset was too drastic to take in a gentle way. It was when I pushed my hat back from my face and took a gaze at the stars that I decided to get up. Pa was pulling back his blankets too. Seeing me, he nodded.

"Know what you mean," I said with a shiver. "It's

too late to get any more sleep and too goddamn cold to go without coffee. You get the Arbuckles and I'll get the fire going."

"Done," I heard him mumble, as he took to rolling his blankets. Ben and Wash looked to be sleeping like babies.

I gathered up what deadwood I could find, realizing that the further south we went, the less likely we were to have deadwood available for our fires. In a way it made me that much more determined to catch up with these yahoos we were chasing. Besides, going without coffee was going to give everyone a sour disposition in the mornings. And I knew that if that happened, we were just as likely to kill one another as the horse thieves. Yes sir, I really was growing to appreciate those Arbuckle brothers.

Kneeling across the fire from Pa, I said, "I'm glad you came along." One of the reasons I'd slept kind of light was the harsh words I'd had with Pa. It wasn't the first time we'd come to blows after I'd come back from the war, and I can't say that I ever felt good about cussing the man who had raised me.

He shrugged. "Everyone needs to air his lungs once in a while." After a moment of silence, he cocked an eye at me and added, "Besides, I make damn good coffee." That was Pa, almost getting sentimental, but never enough so you'd notice it.

"There's that too."

I got Ben and Wash up when the coffee was boiling and we had a fast breakfast before sunup.

"What about these dead bodies?" Wash asked when we were breaking camp.

"Good point, Wash," Ben said, and proceeded to

61

pick one of the dead men clean of his guns and ammunition. When he was through with the man's artillery, he rifled his pockets, both the shirt and the pants.

"Now, Ben, I can see you taking the man's firearms," Wash said in what I thought was a squeamish tone, "but do you think it's necessary to take his money too?"

Ben looked back over his shoulder, cocking an eye at Wash as though the boy were mad. "Tell me something, Wash."

"If I can."

"You ever seen a buzzard pick anything but meat off of a dead man?"

"No sir."

"Well, I not only ain't seen 'em pick dinero off a body, I ain't seen 'em fly into a saloon and order a drink with it either, if it makes you feel any better."

I started going through the pockets of the man whose body I was already stripping of guns and ammunition. Ben had a point and there was no use going back over this bird a second time.

"Man's right, Wash," I said. "If there's a Maker, I reckon He's taking care of his soul. All you got to do is look around to see we already shot up his ass."

Pa, who was now doing the same with his victim, stopped a moment and gave his youngest son his speechifying look.

"You want to ponder on the moral aspect of this, son, I'd suggest you wait until you make it back to Twin Rifles," he said. "Besides, there's a practical matter to be looked after here. I don't figure we've got much more than another day's worth of food left between the four of us. Them four dogs we chased off last night come back, why, they'll do the same thing we're doing. Difference is they'll use the ammunition and extra rifles and pistols to track us down and kill us. What money they find on their compadres, why, they'll use it all up on whiskey. I'd rather live to tell this story, and money is what we're gonna need to get us some food ary we come on a house or a village of sorts."

"Sure, Pa," was all Wash replied with, but I didn't think his heart was in it as he took what he could from one of the dead men, while Pa and Ben and me got the rest of them.

"Don't worry 'bout digging no graves, Wash," Pa said when we were through collecting guns, money, and ammunition. "These men deserve the buzzards that are gonna be pecking away at 'em soon as we leave." It seemed evident that Pa was talking for Wash's sake more than anyone. I knew I had no intention of burying these worthless bastards, and I didn't think Ben was the type to mourn over this type of cutthroat either.

We rounded up about three of their horses and loaded them up with whatever guns and ammunition we couldn't carry ourselves.

"I understand they fed you boys mule at times during that war," Pa said as we mounted up to leave.

"That's a fact," I said.

"God's honest truth," Wash said.

"I'm trying to forget that experience," Ben said.

Pa smiled in that mischievous way he had. "Well,

lads, ary we don't come on a village that's got the food we'll be needing, shortly, you'll have a chance at adding the eating of horseflesh to your list of delicacies," he said.

I didn't think I'd be able to convince my stomach that I was eating a tasty beefsteak when it was actually horse meat I was swallowing. Of course, I remembered the story about those folks in the Donner party who got so bad off they took to eating their own people as they died. Makes a body wonder just how desperate a human can get for food. Yes sir.

We did a good bit of traveling that morning, but I couldn't tell you how far. Maybe it only seemed like a long ways because the morning took a while to pass. I had a lot on my mind. Hell, I'd started out mad at the horse thieves I was chasing, then found myself getting mad at Pa for his way of thinking. With my luck I figured that by sundown I'd have pushed Wash and Ben to the wall too. But damn it, those horses were all me and my brother had going for us and that was important. We had to get those horses back, we just had to!

Somewhere later in the morning, I noticed that the tracks looked fresher than they had been. I was also taking more than my fair share of glances toward the horizons to see if any of Jefe's survivors had gotten up the courage to come after us. So far there had been none.

It was sometime before noon camp, maybe a couple of hours, that we came on a small water hole. I never could figure out what it was that made a body so tired riding a horse. Maybe it was knowing how tired the horse actually was that made you act like you were a mite worn-out too. The four of us took our hats off and ran a sleeve across our brow, for the sun was up and moving on noon. I knew that the next six hours would likely be the hottest of the day. I'd finished scooping up a couple handfuls of water when it hit me, just like that.

It came to me the way things do sometimes, if you know what I mean. You can call it premonition or superstition or anything else that comes to mind, but when it comes to you, why, you'll know what it is those Indian Ghost Dancers put their faith in, that makes believers out of the rest of the tribe.

"Ben, Wash, did that water taste tainted to you?" Pa asked. He might have been looking at Ben and Wash, but when I looked at him he was staring right at me, studying my face as though he'd never seen it before.

"No sir."

"Tasted wet to me, Will," I heard Ben say. "That's the best kind of water, you ask me."

"You thinking or touched, Chance?" I heard Pa ask, but I wasn't sure I wanted to hear him. What was going through my mind seemed much more important at the time.

Abruptly, I turned to my horse and undid the tie on a saddlebag. I didn't have to dig around for I knew exactly where it was and pulled it out immediately. Methodically, I began to check the loads of the second Colt's Army Model .44 now in my hand.

"You expecting trouble, Chance?" Pa was speaking again, cautious like. Now I knew I could answer him, for it had run clean through my mind by now and I knew just what to do.

"Betcherass," I said with a heavy nod. "We're about to come on 'em, Pa. Straight ahead. Soon."

"You want to run that by me again?" Ben asked, a mite confused.

"Ben, the only one who does better on hunches than Chance is me," Pa said, now checking the loads of his Remington. "This boy's had his fair share of 'em in his day, and I'd say most of 'em was right. I never did hear him say it, but I got a strong notion that gut feeling is what got him a good ways through that war of his." Pa winked at Ben. "Chance says he's got a notion, it's best you take heed of it, hoss."

When Ben saw Pa and Wash silently checking their rifles, he shrugged and did the same with his own weapons. "If you say so," he commented.

We rode away from that water hole with full canteens and rifles across our saddles. But we didn't go at a full gallop, instead letting the horses have their heads and half-running, half-trotting in the same direction we had been headed all day.

It was pushing high noon when we came upon it. We hadn't gone but five or six miles, but we came on it as though it were a part of the trail we had been following. Fact of the matter is, the trail led right to the corral and there, by God, were our horses!

The adobe house wasn't small at all. At first glance, I would have said it was a tad bigger than the ranch house we were rebuilding back at Twin Rifles. A fair-size family likely lived in it, if I was any judge of Mexican people. But it wasn't the adobe I was paying all that much attention to as we rode up to the house. Me, I was going over those mounts one by one, trying to see from my horse how much if any damage had been done to them.

A man appeared in the doorway, a handful of small children peeking out from behind him. He was past middle age and had a small, white beard with hair to match and could have been one of those fancy professors if he'd had the clothes and a university standing in back of him instead of the adobe house. Out of the corner of my eye, I saw Ben paying serious attention to a second man who was apparently a hired hand and was in the process of cleaning out the barn, from the pitchfork in his hand. But everything seemed to come to a standstill as we pulled up in front of the man's house.

"Buenas tardes," Pa said, figuring it for at least noon.

"Soon," the Mexican said. "It will soon be afternoon." He put an arm over his forehead and gave a meaningful glance at the sun in the sky. Then he shrugged and smiled back at Pa. "It is close enough not to argue the point."

"You're the first reasonable man I've met in some time," Pa said, giving me a quick glance out of the corner of his eye. "Days are too long to argue 'bout anything."

"Es verdad." He smiled, and added, "My name is Jose. There is water around the side of the casa. You are welcome to it." He paused a moment before his humility began to show. "I'm afraid I only have beans and rice to offer."

"That's right kind of you," I said. "More neighborly than I've seen some folks these past few days. You got a fire, I reckon we can supply some coffee to go with it, if you've a mind."

Jose smiled with what could only be gratitude. I got the impression right off that he was a man who knew manners if nothing else. "That would be most welcome." He smiled again. He soon disappeared back into the adobe structure.

"That's a nice looking herd of horses you've got," Wash said.

Jose shrugged noncommittally. "If you like horses."

By the time we got around to the side, a boy and girl about ten and eleven years of age were scampering back and forth between a well and a fair-size trough, filling it up with bucket after bucket of fresh water.

"Gracias," Wash said. The young ones smiled back at Wash. I reckon he's still young enough to have a face that doesn't scare you the first time you see it. Like I say, you tend to age fast in this land.

"Whoa, now, young 'uns," I said, holding the palm of my hand up for them to stop. Then, in their language, I said, "These horses got their fill a ways back. I reckon we'll be the ones doing most of the drinking this time." It caused them to smile and they set the buckets down next to the trough and waited for us to empty them. I had no doubt that when we were through they would gladly refill the buckets. It crossed my mind that if you came on the right people south of the border, why, they were likely to be just as hospitable as most Westerners.

"Young 'uns got real manners," I said to Pa, after throwing a scoop of water on my face.

"Better than yours ever was, that's for sure."

I thought I heard Wash and Ben laugh but paid little attention to them, instead going back to sloshing water in and around my mouth to cut the dryness I'd been tasting all morning.

We'd managed to get most of the caked dirt off our face and hands and look halfway presentable by the time we were invited into the adobe with the man from the barn. His name was Manuel and he was Jose's brother-in-law. It made sense in a way for families were pretty close down here, and there was too much work to do from can see to can't see to not take on an in-law to help out. Hell, I wouldn't have been surprised if the whole lot of Jefe's gang had been cast out of their individual families as black sheep. It was the piss ugly mean ones who got done that way down here.

You'd have thought we were walking into a church or something, the way we paraded into Jose's home, each of us taking his hat off as we entered. None of us spoke either, but then, I reckon we were all taking in the inside of the adobe house and a mite in awe at what we saw.

From the outside it didn't look much different than any other adobe structure you'd find in this area. But once inside, it was plain to see that this man and his family took great pride in what little they had. The community table they ate at was made of wood that at one time had been polished to hold a shine but was now fading from use. The hardwood chairs were in the same condition, which led me to believe that this was the only home Jose's four children had known.

Rosa was Jose's wife. In her youth I would gauge

that she had been a real beauty, but she was now as middle-aged as Jose and the beauty had faded some. Still, I was betting that she was a woman who knew her way in the world. She smiled when introduced and seemed as friendly as her husband and children.

Pa had unpacked our coffeepot and thrown in a few beans from his sack of Arbuckles. After being introduced, he handed Rosa the coffeepot.

"Ma'am, if you'll fill that with water and set her on the fire till she boils, why, I do believe we'll have a tolerable pot of coffee to drink," Pa said in the same gentle manner he reserved for Ma during her lifetime and, of late, Margaret Ferris back in Twin Rifles. He even bowed deep, the way one of those fellows in a Sir Walter Scott book would do. Seeing Pa act this way was kind of hard to take, after some of the hard spots we'd been in of late.

It was close to half an hour before that coffee was ready, but the smell of rice and beans permeated the house. In the meantime, Wash took to talking to the youngsters while Ben, Pa and me exchanged pleasantries with Jose and Manuel. I don't mind telling you, it all felt a lot easier from the inside of that adobe, where the temperature was a good forty degrees lower than the heat of the day outside.

I was right about Jose and his family. They'd been on this parcel of land a good fifteen years. He didn't give any particulars about the whys and the wherefores, and I didn't ask. For all I knew, he could have inherited the land from Coronado. But right then I didn't care. After all, we were simply passing through.

The fact that we were visitors passing through

70

became disturbingly clear to me when we sat down at the community table to eat. The rice and beans were right tasty and I said so after I'd taken a good mouthful. It was then I looked up and saw that only the four of us and Manuel were eating. Jose and Rosa sat at the table, all right, but all they were doing was sipping at the coffee that had been made. Seated at the end of the table, I was able to take in the rest of the room and the four children sitting in various chairs with rather sad looks on their faces. Oh, they had plates on their laps, but they were empty, as attested by the growling sound I heard from their stomachs.

"Horse apples," I muttered, suddenly feeling like a glutton. The red was crawling up my neck now as I felt thoroughly embarrassed.

"What's the matter?" Rosa said, a look of concern on her face. "Do you not like the food?"

"I love it, ma'am," I said. "I honestly do. Believe me, you set a right fine table."

I got up from the table and took a deep swallow of coffee, which also tasted good.

"What's got into you, Chance?" Ben asked. Both he and Wash and Pa had stopped eating, which was fine with me.

"Miss Rosa," I said. "There's a woman back where I come from by the name of Rachel. She's a right fine cook too. Now, I know that if I went into her kitchen, why, she wouldn't feed me for a week, for that's a woman's domain. Yes, ma'am.

"For all I know, you'll take a knife to me too," I added, "but there's something that's got my curiosity up, so here goes." I stopped talking and made it over

71

to the big pot on the stove in three easy strides. I had to look deep into it to confirm my suspicions, but they proved right.

"Muchachos," I said and waved an arm for the children to come to me. As I suspicioned, they'd only gotten a small scoop of the food we were being served. They willingly held out their plates and I filled them up with a good bit of what was left. They all gave me a grateful *"Gracias"* and went back to their seats.

By this time, Rosa, who was also turning a shade of red at the embarrassment of being discovered, had come over to me.

"Please, senor," she said.

"Get you a couple of plates, ma'am," I said. By now I wasn't in the mood to ask. Hell, I was *telling* her!

"Ma'am, I've been without and it ain't nothing I ever want to go through again," I said as I filled the two plates with the last of the rice and beans. "It's a noble thing to do, ma'am, giving the last of your food to four strangers, but I'll tell you, trading a cup of coffee for it don't seem right to me."

I took the plates from her hand and set them at the table where she and Jose were seated.

"Hospitality is one thing, ma'am, but starving yourself just to show how giving you can be is going a mite too far. I'm sure you'll have no trouble getting past Saint Peter when the time comes, ma'am, but you've got a ways to go before that day."

Since I'd just about taken over the whole place anyway, I figured I'd give a few orders and get the whole thing over with.

"Manuel, I'd like you to do me a favor this afternoon."

"Si, if I can."

"I'd like you to go with Ben, that fellow across the table from you, and show him where you've got suitable eating game around here."

"But, senor, there are chores to be done."

"Don't you worry, Manuel. You're talking to four men who know how to work for a meal. Pa and Wash will take care of that barn of yours in quick order."

"And just what are you gonna do?" Pa asked, a bit uppity.

"Oh, me and Jose will find something to palaver about."

"You through speechifying?" Pa asked when I paused but remained standing.

"In a minute." To Jose and Rosa, I said, "I'd bet a dollar you folks are right religious. I'd bet a second dollar you're used to saying grace."

"Es verdad," Jose said.

"Well, far be it from me to tell you folks what to do in your own home," I said, taking a seat at the table. "Have at it."

So Jose said grace and we went back to eating our rice and beans. But I don't think I was the only one who took my time eating that meal, for all of a sudden it wasn't just a meal. It was a feast of sorts, if you will.

When he wasn't filling his face with food, Pa looked over at me during the meal and shook his head, although I thought I detected a good deal of pride in that look.

"You know, son, I do believe you've got it in you to be a real thoughtful human being. Yes, I do." Pa was letting his pride show and not covering it up the way he usually did.

I waited until my throat cleared, for I suddenly found it hard to swallow, and food didn't have anything to do with it. Maybe it was because I was experiencing one of those moments that you don't often get in life, where one of your kin says something to you that you know you'll never forget. It's the kind of experience that strengthens the bond you already have between you.

I smiled. "There are days, Pa."

CHAPTER

★ 8 ★

If we hadn't been there, I do believe Jose and Rosa and Manuel and the youngsters would have settled down to a good afternoon siesta, the food was that good and that filling. Rosa managed to get the kids to take a nap of sorts, and proceeded to do whatever it was women do between one meal and another in this kind of land. The rest of us were busy in our own way.

Ben and Manuel had taken off to parts unknown in search of food for the pot for the evening meal. I knew they'd come back with something worth eating, for all four of us were feeling the same about taking the last food these people had. I found myself wishing there were more people like Jose and Rosa in the land.

Maybe life would be made a mite easier by the likes of them.

Pa had the good sense to join Wash and finish up the work Manuel showed them he had been doing before the noon meal. I was the one who had been so eager to get the vultures who had stolen the horses me and my brother had made a stake of, so it was only right—at least from my point of view—that I be the one who explained the whole mess to Jose.

"I saw you eye the horses when you came," Jose said when we left the adobe and I wandered over to the corral. "Almost as if they were your very own." He said this last as though he were guessing my purpose in approaching the corral.

"Were I a betting man, Jose, I'd say you come on them horses not long ago," I said, cocking an eye toward the man. I was figuring him for being an honest man as well as a wise one.

"You seem to do a lot of betting, senor," he said with the soft smile of a philosopher.

"Well, if ever there was a land to do it in, this is it," I said, waving an arm to cover the wide expanse of flat land that covered the horizon, no matter in which direction you looked.

"Es verdad," he acknowledged. He must have figured we were on the level of one philosopher talking to another, and maybe we were. Hell, as much time as a man has on his hands out here at times, why, he can't help but make comment on himself and the land around him. He may just be talking to himself at times, you understand, but mostly he'll remember his comments for when he does find someone to palaver with.

"Seems to me it's about time to do some storytelling, Jose," I said, and proceeded to tell the man how I'd come to lose my horses and wound up south of the border looking for them. He took a genuine interest in my words as I spoke, which I purely appreciated. It's an aggravation to tell that long a story and find out you're just flapping your lips for nothing because the other fellow hasn't got nothing between his ears to pick up on what you're saying in the first place. Wasted energy is what it is.

"We tracked 'em all the way from Twin Rifles, and sure enough they wound up here," I said, indicating the herd in the corral. "I recognize most of 'em, and that's a fact, Jose."

"Then by all means, take them back home where they belong," he said in a pleasing way. "As you can tell, I am far from a horseman. And my corral is used only for keeping the few animals I do have."

"I'll do that, Jose," I said. "But I'm also interested in how you happened to come on these animals in the first place. I know there's something to be said for miracles, but you'd have a hard time convincing me these four-legged critters just opened the gate and let themselves in by their own selves."

Jose chuckled. "Hardly, *mi amigo*. The same four men you describe as being thieves brought them here only a day ago."

"Asked you to keep 'em, did they?"

"No. Actually, they threatened to kill me and my family if we did not keep watch over the horses, while they went into the village south of here to enjoy the putas." Now, hoss, in most places I've been a woman is a woman, and you'll find out what their druthers are

77

and their line of work when you come across them. But down in this neck of the woods, why, a whore was a whore, and folks like Jose put enough emphasis on the definition to let you know what they thought about it! Yes sir, those four yahoos had taken to the nearest village to seek out whatever red-light district women they could. But if they were as new to Mexico as I figured, I doubted they'd find what they were looking for all that available.

"Sounds like 'em," I said.

"They came into my house and ate as much as they could before moving on. They had no manners at all, and the children were afraid of them."

"After an experience like that, I'm surprised you took to the four of us when we rode up," I said.

"Believe me, my friend, Manuel had a rifle next to the door of the barn in case you were less than friendly." He smiled.

"What about you? I didn't see you toting any hardware."

Again he smiled. "Sometimes, senor, it is necessary to be like the chameleon in this land."

"Pardon me?" I didn't quite catch the gist of what he was saying.

"There is a reason for wearing such loose fitting clothing in this land, senor. The main reason is that it keeps a man a bit cooler than your close fitting shirts and pants." I was about to ask him to explain further, when he slowly pulled back the oversize sleeve of his left arm, revealing a sheath that was strapped to the inside of his arm. With just the right movement of his forearm, a razor sharp knife slid out into the palm of his right hand. Out of habit, I found myself jumping back, for I was no longer talking to a philosopher but a deadly knife fighter. He took a quick step to his right and tossed the knife, hitting a crossbar of the corral behind me.

"Like the chameleon," he said, "one must sometimes appear different than one is. *Comprende?*"

"Now you're talking my language," I said. He didn't have to say any more, for I knew from experience that most Mexicans never had that much luck when it came to firearms. They either couldn't find the right kind of gunpowder to shoot effectively, or the weapons they had were secondhand and broken-down to begin with. But, hoss, you give one of these fellows something that has a blade to it, why, they were hell on wheels!

"I hadn't worn such a weapon in many a year," Jose said. "But after the revolution started and my home was nearly pillaged, I put it back on. If you had been of the same cloth as the first four men"—here he shrugged with a hint of a smile—"well, senor, I might have died, but I assure you that one of you would accompany me to the graveyard."

"You've made a believer out of me, Jose," I said, and I meant it.

Pa and Wash soon finished up their chores in the barn and I saw Ben and Manuel riding in from a distance about an hour later. During that time, I had been giving serious thought to Jose and his position with the four men we'd been chasing. It seemed about right to give the man an upper hand in case something like this ever happened again.

Ben and Manuel had a handful of birds hanging from their mounts. Jose had a grateful look as he eyed the fowl.

"We will eat well tonight, senors," he said. "You will stay, of course, for supper."

"I don't know, friend," Pa said. "We still got these yahoos we come after to catch up with."

"Don't worry about 'em, Pa," I said. "Like I told you, me and Jose found a few things to palaver about. I already got some designs on those fellas."

"I have too, senor," Jose said. "We will talk of this after the meal tonight." To his brother-in-law, he said, "If you would, Manuel, I would appreciate your giving Rosa a hand with the birds."

I reckon Manuel was conjuring up an appetite looking at those birds, for he consented without an argument.

"I'll give you a hand too, hoss," Wash said. "Who knows, maybe we can rope the young 'uns into helping out."

"The young ones like him," Jose said with a smile, as Wash walked away.

"They ought to," I said. "There're days I recall him acting their age." The comment got a laugh from all three of them, but I figured since I had the floor, I'd get my palavering out of the way.

"Say, Pa, do you think those three mounts we took off Jefe's men are a mite bogged down with all that hardware?" I asked.

"Wouldn't take long to answer that, son. Hell, I figured 'em for swaybacks by the time we get back home. That's a lot of rifles and ammunition we're carrying."

The Long Rope

"That's what I was thinking too."

"Taking them mounts of yours back is gonna be a handful of a job, gents," Ben said. He must have picked up on what I was thinking. "If you plan on taking back the horse thieves that took 'em in the first place, well, you're gonna have a *real* problem. I'd get rid of as much of that hardware as I could before I headed back."

"I see what you mean," Pa said. To Jose, he said, "Amigo, let's get you fixed up proper with some decent rifles and hunting firearms."

And that we did. By the time we were through that afternoon, Jose had in his possession two Henry Rifles, with a hundred rounds of ammunition for them, a good long-barreled shotgun and a couple of Colt's and Remington pistols of .36 and .44 caliber, all with powder, cap, and ball. We threw in a bullet mold for each pistol for good measure.

By the time he got through telling Rosa about his newfound arsenal, why, you'd have thought he was going to war.

And in a way, he was.

CHAPTER ★ 9 ★

Jose was right. The evening meal was a good one and everyone ate their fill. Perhaps that was what made it a good meal. It tends to shame a body when he's shoving food in his face, one fist after another, and there's another person going without, all in the same room. Life shouldn't ever be that way.

To top it off, Jose said grace again, and we all took our time eating those birds. It had been a long time since I'd eaten as slow as I had that day and it set me to thinking. Maybe that was why the folks in this land took their time eating and doing their chores and such. Maybe there was something to this praying before meals. Sort of like a reminder three times a day that a body ought to take to heart what it was he had and didn't have, and enjoy it while he could. I know I sure did appreciate eating the meals I had at the home of this small Mexican family. That's a fact.

"Ma'am, I don't believe I've ever had a bird as tasty as this one," Pa said. "There's a woman back home who'd purely love to have that recipe, ary you'd mind giving it out."

Rosa smiled the way a woman does after she's fed a table full of hungry men and satisfied them all. "It is no bother. I will write it down for your lady friend."

"Yes, ma'am," Pa said, although I thought I saw a bit of red creeping up his neck after hearing Rosa use the term "lady friend." That purely obfuscated Pa. Wash and me knew better than to laugh. Ben too only smiled.

We moved a couple of those hardwood chairs outside and enjoyed the evening as the heat of the day cooled off and the sky soon filled with stars. Having one last cup of coffee made it that much more enjoyable.

"Now then, Jose," Pa said, "you said something about discussing a notion you had?"

"*Si.*" He didn't speak right away, as though formulating his thoughts into the proper words. After a minute, I thought I saw a frown form on Pa's forehead.

"Pa ain't used to waiting that long for an answer, Jose," I said with a grin. "I hope you ain't gonna take all night."

"You Americanos are too much in a hurry. You run here and run there, but seldom rest long enough to enjoy what you work so hard for. It is a shame," Jose said. It was the philosopher coming out in the man, I reckon.

"That's what we do around campfires at night, hoss," Pa said. "Of course, we also do a mite of palavering too, you understand." It was as close to a hint as Pa was going to come, so he was silent then, taking to enjoying the coffee in his cup.

Jose smiled. "I understand." After one more sip of his coffee, he began to explain what he had in mind. He started by explaining to Ben and Pa what he had told me that afternoon, about the yahoos threatening his family and all. Wash was sitting off to the side, being entertained by the two older children, who were teaching him how to play a wooden flute. He was having too much fun to interrupt, so I determined to let him in later on what was going on.

"The gringos will come back to get their horses," he said, "of that I am sure."

"You mean *our* horses," I corrected him.

"Your horses, yes. And when they return, they will be mad, I fear. Mad at each other."

"How's that?" Ben asked, as stumped as the rest of us.

"Because"—Jose smiled—"there is only one puta in the village they go to. And no man likes to share his woman with another man. The woman will tell each she loves him the most and sour their tempers toward one another. I know, for I was young once too."

"Got a helluva memory, I'd say," Pa said.

"It is not memory so much as it is the understanding of man and his ways."

"If you say so," I said with a shrug.

"I am in need of supplies. As I told you, the gringos

84

ate much of my food before you arrived. Tomorrow I will go to the village. There is a store there where I get my supplies. A man runs it with his wife." He smiled reflectively. "She is also the town gossip. She will know what these men have done. When I return, I will let you know their plans. This will help you capture them, I believe. No?"

"I'd say yes." Pa was nodding his head, enthusiastic about the plan.

"Don't you think it would be kind of dangerous?" I asked.

Jose shrugged. "Life is dangerous. I could be bit by a rattlesnake or trampled by a horse."

"Or shot by one of those yellow bastards," Ben said bluntly.

"Manuel will go with me. Besides, the gringos think of me as a poor farmer. They have already had their chance to push me around."

The next morning Rosa fixed up the last of the bacon we had in our saddlebags.

"Mought's well fix it now," Pa told her. "Another day and it'll be on its way to rancid. Besides, I like your cooking."

Rosa obliged and we had another good meal. I was going to be real sad to leave this house and the woman's cooking. Trail cooking would never be the same again, of that I was sure.

It was sunup when Jose and Manuel left in their buckboard to head for town. But before they left, Pa and I approached them with a couple of twenty dollar gold pieces we'd taken from the dead men in Jefe's bunch of toughs.

"Look, Jose, we're gonna be needing some supplies

EX-RANGERS

when we head back to Texas," I said. "I don't know what all that supply man of yours carries, but I'd appreciate it if you'd pick up some for us."

"You get a couple, three sacks of rice and an equal amount of beans, you understand?" Pa said, his authority showing. "We're heavy eaters, you know."

Jose blushed some. "I understand." I reckon he knew Pa was wanting to get him a healthy amount of food for his table in return for the small amount we'd had. But then, I reckon that's what you call neighborly, no matter what part of the world you happen to be in.

"And some hard rock candy, Jose," Wash said. "Why, with what you've got, you oughtta be able to get six months worth and have enough to store for Christmas to boot."

"You are too kind, senor."

Wash shrugged, grinned. "That's found money, Jose. You best spend it while you can, 'cause that's what found money's best used for. The only thing we're giving up is the spending of it, and it'll do you folks much better than us. Besides, with that hard rock candy, why, you'll have a real hold on those youngsters."

"You have brought your sons up well, my friend Will," Jose said in as earnest a manner as I'd ever heard anyone propose friendship in my lifetime.

Pa said, "Well, I tried, amigo, I tried."

Then they left, and I found myself saying a little prayer to the Maker to watch over them and keep them from harm. I felt a sudden flush run through me, because the whole idea of prayer was quite foreign to me. Then I felt Pa's strong hand on my shoulder.

86

"Don't worry, son," he said. "I done the same thing. 'Tain't nothing to be ashamed of, especially out here." It was sometimes amazing what a father and son shared with one another just by gut feeling. It must be something in the blood. At any rate, I didn't feel embarrassed about what I'd done anymore.

"I reckon we'd best get some work done while they're gone," Ben said. "Won't get done by its ownself."

"Good thinking, Ben," I said. "Wash, you seem to be having a good time with them youngsters. Why don't you keep an eye on 'em while Pa and me tend to the horses?" My brother quickly agreed and was gone with the children.

"I'll find me a shady spot and keep an ear to the ground for riders," Ben volunteered. It sounded like he was trying to get out of work, but I knew that although he wouldn't be working up any blisters, he would still be looking out for our welfare, and that was as necessary as getting the place cleaned up. Maybe more so.

Pa and me set to work feeding and rubbing down the horses as best we could. But I'll tell you, son, it sure did seem like a long morning. I could make a claim that it was the work that was hard, but I'd been brought up on hard work, so to say as much would be a lie. No sir, it was the waiting that was making everything take so long. I knew Pa was feeling the same, and seeing Wash and Ben every once in a while, well, they seemed right restless too. I reckon Pa was right when he said that worrying was sort of like one of those play rocking horses; keeps you busy, it does, but you never get a damn thing done. That's a fact.

"You're looking about as worried as I feel," I said to Rosa about midmorning, when Pa and I took a break and got a dipper of water from the back of the house. Rosa had come out for some water too and we both got to the well at the same time.

"I know. Something tells me there will be trouble."

"Don't you worry, ma'am," Pa said. "We'll take care of you and yours ary there is." To me he added, "I'm gonna tell Wash to take the young 'uns inside when he hears riders coming. He can do a fine job of watching out for 'em if there is trouble."

"Sounds good," I said as Pa turned to leave. "It'll ease my mind too." I don't know why, but I had an awful awkward feeling within me then, standing there alone with Rosa. I sensed that she was feeling the same.

"He is a very caring man, your father," she said.

"He has his moments." I smiled.

"I want you to know that I am glad you and your friends have come. The children love Wash, and Jose has not had another man to speak to other than my brother for a long time."

"Ma'am, I'm proud to call you and Jose friends."

I slapped on my hat and excused myself, saying I had to get back to work, even though most of what needed being done had already been taken care of.

"You look red in the face, boy," Pa said when I got back to the barn and the horses.

"It's the heat, Pa."

Ben gave out a short whistle from the near side of the house that got our attention. Silently, he motioned toward the back of the house, the same direction that Jose and Manuel had taken when heading for the village. Once he had silently informed us what was going on, he ducked around the corner and told Wash. It didn't take but ten seconds before my brother had those youngsters out of sight and inside the adobe house.

Pa and me squinted in the distance and each made up our mind that it was safer to get out of sight. At first we could hear the buckboard coming, but it was the sight of five horsemen accompanying it that made us real cautious.

"It appears our plan has backfired some, Chance," I heard Pa say as we ducked into the barn.

From the looks of it, Pa was right. Garver, Handy, and Quartermain were riding up with Jack Terrence, alongside a rather complacent Jose and Manuel, seated on the buckboard. A fifth man was riding with them, a big plug ugly I didn't know from Adam. Two things crossed my mind as I watched the riders near us. The first was that Pa was right, that our plan had backfired and we were in trouble. After all, these men could have seen Jose loading up more than his usual amount of supplies and caught on to what he was doing. The second was that Jack Terrence had picked up an additional man to help him out and they had come back to get the horses and hadn't discovered what they were walking into yet. One thing was for sure, there was a fight coming once Terrence and his men saw Wash or me. Truth to tell, I was feeling that mad come back to me for the fool these yahoos had me look like. Hell, they'd stolen my goddamn horses!

"Rosa, put the rice and beans on," Jose yelled when he pulled his team to a halt. "Our gringo friends are here again."

Hearing that, I knew he was letting his wife know of the danger that lay in store for her. I also knew that he was expecting trouble too. That slight knowledge helped me make up my mind.

The big ugly one had come up on my side of the buckboard with Jack Terrence between him and Manuel. My mind was working fast now, a plan quickly forming. Mind you now, I was in a land where you usually gave a man a chance to have at you, if you wanted to fight fair and square. But I'd come from a war that was anything but fair, and had no intention of giving any of these pilgrims a chance to do more than they already had to me.

"Cover me, Pa," I said, as I stepped out in the middle of the barn door, my Colt's .44 in hand. "You boys just drop your guns and don't try nothing stupid." I had the Colt's leveled at Plug Ugly, since he was the only one who had a rifle laid across his saddle. He was also nearest to me. The rest of the riders had their rifles holstered underneath their saddles. The riders on the far side of the buckboard were counting the horses to see if they were all still there, while Jack Terrence was looking about for more guns and hiding places.

There were two seconds of full silence, all of which was too long for me. That was giving them time to think, and I didn't want that, so I cocked my pistol to let them know I meant business. When I did, Plug Ugly decided it was time to call my bluff and began moving that rifle toward me. I shot him in the chest and he went flying back over the rear of his saddle.

"That was stupid," I said.

Pa had stepped out beside me and leveled his rifle at

Jack Terrence, shooting his pistol from his hand before he could put it to use. In fact, Terrence wasn't having much of a day at all. Plug Ugly had brought his rifle up into the air as he slid off the back of his mount, letting go of his rifle as he did. The rifle flew back into Terrence's face just as Pa's bullet stung his wrist and hit him from the blind side.

Manuel, nearest to him, saw his chance and took it, jumping Terrence and tumbling to the ground on top of him. He got in a couple of good blows to the man's face before the big man got up and decided to play hell with Manuel. Meanwhile, Pa had moved around to the back of the man, who was now filled with rage, apparently forgetting or not caring that we were armed.

"Hey, mister!" he yelled as Terrence had bloodied Manuel's mouth some. Terrence, annoyed, began to turn to his rear, an angry look about him. It was obvious that he didn't like being disturbed when he had the upper hand in a fight. But all he saw was the butt of Pa's rifle before it smashed into the side of his face like some boulder rolling down on top of him. Manuel moved out of the way so the big man didn't fall atop him when he hit the dust. Like I said, Jack Terrence wasn't having a good day at all.

The horses of Plug Ugly and Terrence had gotten real skittish at the sound of gunfire and had moved out of the way. I'd gotten so interested in the fight between Manuel and Terrence that I had clean forgotten about Plug Ugly. The man was gut shot but not yet dead.

"Chance!" I heard Jose yell in warning. He was pulling out that throwing knife of his when Plug Ugly

91

came back to mind. By the time I glanced down at the man, I was cocking my pistol and bringing it up to him again. But before I could get a decent aim, I saw Jose's knife stuck deep in the man's chest, right over the heart. Plug Ugly had just pulled his pistol and was about to kill me in cold blood. His shot went wild as his hand fell to the ground, forcing the six-gun to fire as it hit the ground.

That near an experience with dying made me remember real quick that there were still three more members of this gang I hadn't heard from. But it was too late, for when I looked up they all had their guns drawn as well.

"You can die stupid like your friends just did, or live just feeling dumb, boys," Wash said. He'd stepped out the front door of the adobe and had his Dance Brothers pistol trained on Garver, Handy, and Quartermain, who were on his side of the buckboard. I could see that the three of them were giving serious consideration to trying to gun down my brother, for there were three of them and only one of him.

"Don't even think it, friend," I said, taking quick aim at Quartermain, who was closest to me, well within pistol range.

"Time to fish or cut bait, boys," I heard Pa say as he jacked a round into his rifle and took aim at Handy in the middle.

All that was left for these boys was to turn tail and run, but they couldn't even do that. Garver looked over his shoulder, only to see Ben standing in back of all of them with a scatter-gun in hand.

"You don't want to do that, gents," he said in dead earnest. "These here shotguns make an awful mess, especially if you live to tell about it. Of course, in that case you'd be too ugly for anyone to want to be around."

"I think I would very carefully give them my guns if I were you," Jose said. Lordy, but that man was good with words and a smile, both of which were evident now. Yes sir, wise words they were. If the three able-bodied riders weren't listening to anyone else that day, they heard Jose's words and stripped themselves of their weapons.

The children all gathered around Wash as the three remaining horse thieves dismounted. But it was clear that Wash wasn't at all concerned about hero worship. If anything, he was as mad as I was about catching up with these men.

Garver had a crooked smile on his face as he got down from his horse, and that set off Wash. He took a long stride toward the man, holstering his pistol as he did, and let out a long, roundhouse swing that landed on Garver's jaw and flattened him like a dropped piece of lead. Pepe, Jose's oldest boy, grimaced as he saw the man fall, a trickle of blood flowing from his mouth.

"Don't ever lie to a man and don't ever steal, Pepe," Wash said in a serious manner. "Falling in with the wrong crowd and stealing will get you killed. Lying will get you knocked flat on your ass." He pointed at Garver, who was just coming to. "That's how you'll wind up, and I guarantee it hurts something fierce." The pain had finally caught up with Wash and he was shaking his fist. I thought I saw Jose raise his eyebrows, thoroughly impressed with Wash's action and words and the impression they had made on his son.

"Gents," Ben said, "it looks like we got another mess to clean up."

CHAPTER

★ 10 ★

The humanity in Jose demanded that Plug Ugly get a decent burial, so Pa, Jose, and I spent a good portion of the afternoon digging a grave for the dead man out behind the barn.

"How come you're burying him back here?" I asked, about halfway through the digging.

Jose smiled shyly. "Next spring I will know where to plant my garden."

Pa glanced down at the dead man. "I reckon that is a good chunk of fertilizer, ain't it?"

It was while we dug the grave that Jose filled us in on what had happened in the village. Terrence and his men had spotted Jose and Manuel in the small village and had gotten suspicious, because of all the supplies they were loading up, and because of the money they were paying for the supplies with. No dirt farmer like Jose had that kind of money, or should have.

"It was their greed which brought them out here again," Jose said. "They thought I must have hidden more of this dinero and kept it from them before." He shook his head. "Greed is a terrible thing."

"Ain't that the truth," Pa said.

Rosa had cleaned up Manuel, who had then joined Ben for another afternoon of hunting. When they returned, we had just finished planting Plug Ugly. Once again, they had three or four good-size birds with them. Rosa assured us she would have no trouble making a bountiful evening meal, even for the prisoners.

Wash had been keeping an eye on our horse thieves, who were now securely bound. The only favor Wash did them was to place them in the shade that afternoon.

"Jose was right," he said when Rosa drew some water for us early in the afternoon. "All these birds are doing is arguing about who had the most manhood." Wash had the foresight to make sure that Rosa was out of sight and sound before making that statement.

"Let 'em have at it," I said. "Sounds like they'll spend the rest of the day keeping one another exhausted just by flapping their lips."

"Only sweat they're gonna work up is on their upper lip," Pa said. "And here we are, digging a grave for their partner." I had a notion that, to Pa, the situation had taken an ironic twist. Perhaps he was right too.

Hell, we'd caught the horse thieves and they were still having the easy life.

Pa took to keeping an eye on the horse thieves while Wash and I helped Jose unload the sacks of beans and rice. We also unloaded some jerked beef and Indian bread, which wasn't half bad if it was anything like what I remembered tasting.

Killing never did do anything for my appetite, so we worked on through the noon meal and worked up an appetite for the supper meal Rosa was making for us. When it came, it sure was tasty. Or maybe it was just my stomach growling that made it seem tasty.

After we finished the meal, I noticed Pepe helping Wash feed the prisoners. I had to look twice when I saw Terrence, for there was something familiar about him that I still couldn't figure out. It was one of those things that sticks way in the back of your mind and will come out only when it's good and ready, if you know what I mean. Still, it bothered me. Had I known him during the war? Possibly. Hell, thinking back on it, why, there must have been a million men fighting that war on both the North and South sides. But what were the odds that you'd meet one of them out here after the war was over? On the other hand, how wouldn't I meet one of them out here after the war? I remembered seeing people heading for Texas like there wasn't any tomorrow, when I'd left the army a few months back. If that was any indication, why, half of the armies of the North and South could be trying to make a life in Texas by now. A scary thought crossed my mind then: What if there was some truth to that and the people moving down here didn't get along and we started fighting the War Between the

States all over again? I didn't think I was ready for that!

"I suppose you will be leaving soon to go back to your ranch," Jose said when we'd settled down in the hardwood chairs again.

"Likely tomorrow, I'd say," I said. "What do you think, Pa?"

"Sounds good to me. I'll have to check on Joshua and see ary he's had any more takeovers from those carpetbagging Yankees."

I chuckled, remembering the fix Joshua had gotten into the last time the three of us had left Twin Rifles and returned when our mission was finished.

"The children will miss Wash," Jose said in a tone that sounded as though it had a bit of melancholy to it. "Rosa will miss cooking for you." He paused and thought a moment. "And I will miss our conversations. They have been most pleasurable, my friends."

"Well, I feel the same about you, Jose," Pa said.

"That goes for me too," I said. I think Pa and I knew how much Jose meant his words. I'm also pretty sure that Jose knew how much we meant what we said. Sometimes it ain't the words you say but the quality of them that gets across your meaning. A lot of times you don't need more than that and this was one of those times.

We spent maybe an hour talking of this and that and taking interest in each other's words and thoughts. Easy times like that at the close of the day are some of the most enjoyable.

When Jose turned in, Pa and Ben and I were still sitting outside, joined by Wash. Ben had been quiet all night, but Pa brought him into the conversation.

"What's your plans, Ben?" he asked in a casual way. "Or have you got any plans?"

"Why, shoot, I reckon I'll have to at least get you boys back to the border with these yahoos and them horses," he said in a blustery way. "Lucky I come along to save your hide."

"Can't deny that," Pa said with a rare smile.

"What about Shelby and that war you was heading for?" I asked.

Ben shrugged, smiled. "Hell, it's been going on as long as the War Betwixt the States was. I reckon it'll still be there a week from now."

"Good," I said. "Now that you've got that settled, who's gonna take the first watch?" We still had prisoners to watch over and I didn't trust them worth spit.

"Might as well be me, son," Pa said.

"Age before beauty, huh?"

"Hell, no!" he said, as though I'd ruffled his feathers. "Someone's got to be awake enough in the morning to put on the coffee!"

CHAPTER

★ 11 ★

Rosa cooked us one last good meal the next morning before we left. I reckon she knew we'd be going back to eating our own cooking until we got back to Twin Rifles, so the meal was especially good.

We'd been up early, saddling and watering the horses and filling as many extra canteens as we could carry with us, to include the prisoners. Given my druthers, I wouldn't feed those birds until we got back to Twin Rifles, but they had to ride too, so that was four more horses we had to take care of on the ride back. Who knows, maybe being around Jose and his family was making me a mite more religious about life.

Pa and I had discovered that Jose was feeding the herd of horses with the last bit of grain he had too, so we made note of it and handed him three more double eagles before we left.

"You'll have to buy more grain to feed your animals, hoss," Pa said with a wink.

"You are most generous, senors," Jose said. He looked at the four prisoners, who were now sitting on horseback, hands tied to their saddles, and grinned. "It seems that I now do have the *mucho dinero* the gringos perceived me to have."

Rosa appeared in the doorway. I glanced at her and smiled.

"Jose, Rosa," I said, "a man don't get a chance to find much better friends than you folks. You ever find yourself between a rock and a hard spot, you send word our way and we'll come a-running."

"We're burning daylight, gents," Ben said. "We still got a ways to go to the border."

"One other thing, senors," Jose said.

"Better make it fast," I said. "Ben's getting antsy."

"You did not mention them in your adventures across the border, so perhaps you have not come across them yet."

"Them?" Pa asked.

"The Kickapoo. Everyone is concerned about Juarez and his men near the border, but they forget about the Kickapoo."

The Kickapoo had once lived along the Kaw River in Kansas. Their tribe had been thrown into total confusion by the War Between the States and the skirmishes that took place by both the North and the South, especially those during the years before the war when their homeland had been known as "Bloody Kansas." When both sides tried to get the Kickapoo to take sides with them in the war, the tribe refused. The war had swept through their homelands and left little islands of Indians here and there and, from what I gathered, left them only one choice. By 1864 the tribe was faced with the threat of starvation and disease, all of which followed a number of cold winters when their lands had been ravaged by not only Mother Nature but outlaws and bandits. There might have been all of four hundred men, accompanied by their women and children, who then decided to leave the territory of the United States.

I reckon they were an early version of Shelby and his men, for they fled south toward Mexico. Unfortunately, they left one war for another when they did, but at least they were able to set up a piece of land where they could live in relative peace. The government of Maximilian gave them a land grant. The boundaries weren't the best that had ever been defined and were located in the arid Santa Rosa Mountains, just south of the Rio Grande.

I remembered that you could just barely see the Santa Rosa Range on the way down here, but that didn't mean anything. Hell, I'd known Indians who had grown up in this land who could travel for longer than most humans thought possible, and do it on less than a canteen of water. I reckon that was one of the things that most folks forgot about when they entered this land. It wasn't really theirs to begin with. Shoot, son, the people in this nation had spent nearly a hundred years exploring what they called the North American continent, and that was before the War

Between the States. But the war had changed everything and now it seemed like everyone and his brother
was headed west to make a new start. I had a notion
that the mass of people heading west of the Mississi-
pi were going to settle this land, or die trying. That
was where they made their biggest mistake, thinking
that the land was all free for the taking. I knew that
some of them would likely die with that thought in
mind.

Jose had been right. I'd had my mind on Juarez and
his band of riders and forgotten all about the Indian
element in this land. Shows you what can happen
when you get downright distracted like I had.

"Thanks for that information, Jose," I said. "I
reckon I got so taken with catching these yahoos that I
forgot about anything else."

The children were suddenly out of the house and
surrounded Wash on his horse.

"This is for you, Wash," Pepe said, and handed my
brother a wooden flute much like his own.

"Well, now, I really appreciate that," Wash said.
"I'll practice those lessons you gave me."

"And I will practice what you have taught me," the
boy said. He didn't specify what it was, but I had a
healthy notion that he had taken to heart Wash's
warning about lying, killing, and falling in with the
wrong company.

"You are a caring man, Will Carston," Rosa said,
and handed him a small flat box. "Such a man should
have this. It will give you guidance and help what you
call your Maker watch over you."

"Well, I'll be," Pa said, opening the box and seeing a
rosary with a cross the size of the box laying on top of

it. "Thank you, ma'am, I'll keep that in mind." He put the box inside his left shirt pocket, behind the badge I knew he had pinned to the inside of that pocket.

"I can only wish you well, Chance," Rosa said, and pulled my arm down to her level and planted a kiss on my cheek. I could feel the flush rushing to my face as she said, "You have the best of the world. A fine brother and a caring father. I can only wish that you become more like them."

"I'll miss you all," I said and I meant it.

"Well, I'm glad you all got that out of the way," Ben said, a bit perturbed, I thought, because he hadn't been given any presents. "We still got a ways to go and that much less time to do it in."

"Oh, but we hadn't forgotten you, *mi amigo,*" Jose said.

"Es verdad," Manuel said, from the other side of Ben's horse. "We thank you for your hunting prowess. It will be sorely missed. Here," he said, and handed what looked like an oversize pocket flask to Ben. "The patron and I make it ourselves. It will warm you in the night chill. Perhaps not as well as a good woman, but it is warmth and it is needed on occasion."

"That's right neighborly, Manuel, Jose," Ben said. He offered his hand to both men, who took it in sincerity. "Like the Carstons said, you ever need a hand, you just give a holler and I'll come a-running."

Then we left.

CHAPTER
★ 12 ★

I knew it was going to take longer getting back than it had coming down because of the horses and the added task of taking care of the prisoners. Garver, Handy, and Quartermain had been sufficiently scared of Ben's shotgun that they gave us little trouble as we headed back home. It was Jack Terrence that kept me wondering when a break was going to come. He just had that attitude that some men do that said he was cocky enough to try damn near anything. It wasn't that it bothered me all that much. Hell, I think both Terrence and me both knew that if he made a break for it, I'd kill him deader than a doornail. It was just one more burr under my saddle that I'd have to put up with for damn near a week.

While Ben kept an eye on the prisoners, Pa and Wash and me did our best to keep the herd of horses under as much control as we could. We found out a lot about what we should know to control a herd of horses—even twenty of them—and a lot about what we shouldn't be doing on that trip. But that turned out to be the least of our worries.

As it turned out, Jose was right about the Kickapoo. I don't know how we missed them on the way down, maybe the presence of Jefe's wild bunch kept them away, but they sure did make themselves known to us on the way back. Of course, we didn't have a herd of horses with us on the way down either. That might have been why they showed up on the horizon close to noon of the second day. We were back on water and hardtack at noon, along with a piece or two of that jerked beef Jose had provided us with. But then, I reckon Wash had gotten used to it as much as I had in the army, so it couldn't have bothered him more than me. I couldn't have cared less about the horse thieves we were transporting back. Still, they had noticed the Indians too, and it worried them.

"You see them redskins?" Terrence asked at noon camp that day.

"That's a fact," I said.

"What're you gonna do about 'em?" Handy asked. He had a look of concern about him. Hell, all four of them had that look. But I'd a notion that if I didn't give them some answers and explanations, why, they'd be plum worried to death by the time we broke camp.

"Where's Wash?" I asked Pa.

"Out watching the herd."

"Good enough," I said. "I'll explain it to him later. Why don't you boys hunker down here a minute and we'll have a war council."

It didn't take but ten minutes to iron out what I had in mind, and no one objected to it at all. I got word to Wash when we broke camp, explaining the situation and my plans to him.

"That's an awful big gamble for our lives and a small herd of horses," he said, not thoroughly convinced of my plan. "How many of them Kickapoo, do you reckon?"

"Twenty-five, maybe thirty," I said. I don't believe any of us had enough time, or the desire, to stand still and get an exact count of how many Kickapoo we were dealing with. Moving targets are a lot harder to hit than a body sitting still.

"You trust these fellas that much, do you, Chance?" my brother asked. "They stole our horses, you know."

"From what I've seen today, little brother, I'd say we're gonna be fighting for a mite more than horseflesh by this afternoon. With the odds stacked against us at four-to-one, we're gonna be fighting for our lives. Gits down to that, why, I always figured a body oughtta have a chance to save his own life, don't you?"

"I'll go along with you, Chance," Wash said in a bothersome way, "but I ain't gonna feel comfortable about it, not at all."

He wheeled his horse and went back to tending the horses as we moved out.

Pa always made a point of telling us over and over again that you have to watch your back trail. "Things look different when you're going in the opposite direction," he said. He was right. Most of the time, Pa was always right. Of late, I'd found myself appreciating that.

It was paying off for me now that we were headed back home to Twin Rifles. I knew that the Kickapoo weren't trailing us just to be taking a pleasure ride. Hell, nobody likes eating dust that much. Showing up when we had a herd of horses led me to believe they were after the horses. It was that simple. And in order to get the horses, they were going to have to attack us some time or another.

What I had in mind was leading them into what was almost a self-made trap, if you will. And, if memory served me correct, we'd run across it during the afternoon.

There was a coulee, a small ravine of sorts, that we had crossed when chasing Terrence and his gang. When I'd spoken to them at noon, they had remembered it as well as I did. The coulee was deep enough for a distance so that no one could get shot, especially the horses, if you were to run them hard down that area. If we could divert the attention of the Kickapoo, I was sure that we'd be able to get away with the horse herd intact. Better yet, if we could lay a bit of our firepower into those Indians, I was certain they would maintain a healthy distance between us and them the rest of the way home. I remembered being stung by a bee when I was a youngster, and it made me shy away from the area the bee's nest was located in for quite some time. I was hoping the same would be true of what I had in mind now.

I rode up next to Terrence and his men later on in the afternoon. It was hot again and we weren't pushing the horses as hard as we had during the morning. There would be time enough for them to run this afternoon.

"Remember what I told you, boys," I said. "You're gonna have two shots apiece, so you'd better make 'em count. Help get us out of this fix and I might even say a few good words at your trial."

"Hell, I'm surprised you ain't hung us yet," Terrence said in his flannelmouthed way. He was getting to be a real bothersome burr under my saddle, yes sir.

"Believe me, Terrence, the thought crosses my mind now and then," I said. "But tell me, pilgrim," I added, waving a hand throughout the expanse of flat land surrounding us, "do you see a tree I can throw a rope over anywhere in sight?"

A wicked smile came to Terrence's face. "No, I don't."

"For what it's worth, I want you to know my brother doesn't take to this idea, so I was you I'd keep in mind to point them rifles at the Kickapoo when you pull the triggers. Besides, he made it through the war with that Shelby general of yours."

"Carston, we all made it through that war," Terrence said with a sneer. A frown came to my face, for I was really getting tired of hearing this man run his mouth.

"Terrence, if you ain't careful, you're gonna have to worry more about spitting your teeth out than you will be about shooting any Indians this afternoon." If

109

I said it hard and mean it was because I meant it that way. But Terrence only guffawed at my words.

"You wouldn't do that." He laughed. "You're one of those—"

My left fist shot out, landing square beneath his nose and a mite to the left. But it was hard enough to jolt him backward, and if he hadn't grabbed hold of his saddle horn, why, he'd have fallen ass over teakettle off his horse.

"I killed a man back there for doing something stupid, Terrence," I said through gritted teeth. "Don't make me kill you for doing something stupid too. Best thing you can do is keep your mouth shut. Get the drift?"

He didn't say anything. Hell, he didn't have to! There was death in his eyes and it was all aimed right at me. I could tell he was wanting to finish this fight, and in the back of my mind I made a note to do just that. As it turned out, I'd have to wait a while.

"Here they come!" I heard Wash yell from the far side of the herd. The horses had been moving along at a leisurely pace, not running at a full trot or walking, but loping along at their own speed. In this heat you couldn't blame them. But now there was a renewed spirit in them as Wash and Pa quickened the pace. Wash was right; behind us a good half mile was the band of renegade Indians and they were headed straight for us.

"Come on," I said to Terrence and his men, "we've got a mile or so to go before we reach that coulee. You know what to do."

I worked the flank of the herd, while Ben was far

ahead. He already had orders on what to do and was proceeding accordingly. I had a notion he had been a good soldier . . . when he had been a soldier. What I had Ben doing was getting down to that coulee before the rest of us. When the horses entered the coulee, he would turn them in one direction or the other, whichever would look best for giving the horses a run to safety. As long as he could keep the leader going in the right direction, I figured that the depth of the ravine would keep the horses from going in any direction but one. Ben's job was to keep them going, hopefully far enough so the Indians wouldn't catch up with him or the horses.

In the meantime, the rest of us would make a stand of sorts just inside the coulee and make believers out of these Kickapoo. It was there that Terrence and his men would play an important part in convincing the renegades that it wasn't wise to tangle with us.

One of the big things the commanders on both sides of the war based their victories on was the effect of strength in numbers. It has one hell of an effect on you if you're going up against a whole passel of guns, rather than one or two. In our case, I figured it would seem an awful lot scarier to these Indians if they were facing seven rifles instead of just three. And hell, we had the rifles galore! After leaving a small arsenal with Jose and the horse that went with it, we now only had two horses with extra pistols, rifles, and ammunition.

But I planned on playing it safe. I planned on putting a couple of Spencers in reach of each of our horse thieves, one on each side of us as we made our stand at the coulee. I chose the Spencer rifle because, although you could eject a used shell and place a new one in the chamber by working the lever under the trigger, it took a full hand to bring the rifle to full cock. As close as my prisoners had their hands tied, I doubted that they would be able to do much more than fire the rifles once. They would have to settle the rifle across the left arm to steady it once they were about to fire, but I'd seen one-armed men in combat who had done quite well with the weapon. Besides, the idea was to give these Indians the notion that we had more firepower than we actually had. Who knew, maybe it would work.

When we came on the coulee, the horses made it down the slope without any trouble. Ben turned the leader to the left and began leading him up the ravine. Deep as it was, it sure didn't look like the place to be when a flash flood hit the area. Pa and Wash helped turn the horses as they entered the coulee, then dismounted.

Meanwhile, Terrence and his men pulled up beside me and slid off their horses. I had to work fast, for the Indians would soon be upon us, and then hell would be paying a visit. By the time I had pulled four more Spencers from our extra horses, Terrence and his men had each pulled the Spencer from the saddle boot of their horses and had spread themselves out along the southern embankment of the coulee. I cocked and placed next to each man an additional Spencer.

Suddenly, the air was full of arrows and I knew what it was like being on the ass end of a porcupine when he got mad.

"Aim for a lead horse!" I yelled at Terrence and his men. Hell, it was easier to hit and could do just as much damage as knocking a brave off his mount, if not more.

Terrence and his men fired first as Pa, Wash, and I took up positions and readied our own rifles. I reckon we were an odd bunch when it came to rifles. I had a Spencer, Pa had a Henry, and Wash toted one of those Colt Revolving Rifles. The only advantage I could see in using such a rifle was that the flash in the pan of that rifle could be right distracting.

Three of the Spencers hit their mark, while one missed. But you wouldn't see me making a check to see who had missed. Two horses had tumbled end over end, throwing their riders. The third shot had killed one of the lead braves. But these were Indians we were dealing with and they were used to fighting to the death. The two who had gotten their ponies shot out from under them just kept on coming, rolling over in a somersault and running toward us.

"Use them long guns, boys!" I yelled and stood up, a Colt in each hand. I made quick work of the running braves, who were dead by the time they hit the ground, praying all the time that Pa and Wash would put out enough gunfire to do away with some more of the ones rushing toward us.

They did.

At least eight of those braves weren't brave anymore. They were dead. Pa and Wash had dusted six of them that first rush.

It turned some of the war party away, but others were not discouraged. Four more had lost their mounts by tripping over a couple dead horses. I don't know if it was embarrassment or pure insanity that drove them, but on they came. Of course, I reckon they weren't the only ones who had gone a mite mad that day. I stood up like a damn fool and cut all four of them to ribbons, not ducking back down until an arrow took my hat from my head. Truth to tell, that scared the hell out of me!

"Reloading!" I yelled, ducking down out of sight.

"Like hell!" Pa yelled back at me. "We ain't got the time! Pull something off of that horse!"

He was right and I grabbed a couple of six-guns from one of the horses with all our extra weaponry. It was milling about, likely not running because there was no place to run to. Besides, if you had that much armory on you, why, I doubt you'd be able to run either.

The gunfire let up some and so did the arrows. I holstered my empty guns and ran toward Terrence and his men, cocking the Spencers for them again.

"Nice shooting," I said, breathless.

"Betcherass," Terrence growled. I gave him a hard look but didn't have the energy to argue with him.

"Keeping up your shooting eye, Pa?" Wash said, laying his revolving rifle aside for a freshly loaded Henry.

"Can't afford not to now that you two are around," Pa said.

I smiled briefly at my brother. "Ain't changed a bit, has he?"

Wash smiled back. "I hope not."

They came at us a second time, and I got a real surprise.

"Gimme that thing!" Handy yelled and grabbed a Remington from my left hand. At first I thought he was going to shoot me, but he didn't. When I looked, I saw him running away from me down toward the east end of the ravine. It made my blood boil to see a man running away like that.

"Sorry sonofabitch!" I mumbled to myself and ran after him.

It wasn't until I'd almost caught up with him that I saw what he was really doing. And by then it was too late. A half-dozen warriors had decided to come at us from the side, riding through the coulee at us from the east. Apparently, Handy was the first and maybe the only one to see them. He couldn't use the Spencer on them with any effect, so he'd grabbed a pistol from me and now stood there in full view, shooting three of the six out of their saddles before falling backward. He was dead by the time he fell to the ground, three or four arrows in his chest.

I did my best to sidestep the three empty ponies as they rushed past me, but surprised the hell out of the remaining warriors as I appeared in front of them in the dust and gunsmoke. I shot two of them out of their ponies and the third one in the back as he raced past me. Seeing Handy laying there dead sent a rush of hatred through me. Oh, the man had stolen my horses, there could be no denying that. But he had died helping to defend our position. I placed a quick second shot in each of the three men I had killed and looked about quick like for any more surprise attacks.

Then the gunfire died down a second time, all except for some distant rifle fire. When I got back to Pa, the Kickapoo were running away, a far lesser force than when they had first decided to steal our horses

115

and kill us to boot. Off to the west I thought I identified Ben, standing his ground and shooting his rifle at the Kickapoo as they retreated.

"Count 'em out and I'd say we thinned their ranks by a good twenty," Pa said with a nod, quickly reloading his Henry. I had a notion that the barrel of his rifle was hot enough to brand cattle with.

"Handy's dead," I said, indicating the location of his body. "Looks like he was a good man, after all."

"It's a shame," Wash said.

I walked over to Terrence, who still looked as mean as ever. It made me wonder if killing didn't make him all the meaner.

"You boys did a damn good job," I said. "I'm glad we had you along. You made a difference. Like I said, I'll make note of it when we get back. It'll go in your favor."

I stuck the Remington in my waistband and started breaking down my Colt's to reload it with a fresh cylinder. It was as though I had forgotten about the rest of the world, but it wasn't for long.

"I ain't going back, Carston," Terrence said in his gravelly voice. I reckon everyone thought someone else had an eye on him, but we all made the mistake of reloading our weapons at the same time. It was then that Terrence had grabbed up that Spencer and now had it pointed at me.

"You did a good job, Terrence," I said, getting perturbed at the sight of the rifle. "Don't foul it up now. Put that damn thing down."

"Oh, no, I ain't going back."

"He claims to have killed men," Quartermain said,

a Spencer in his hand too, although it wasn't aimed at anyone.

"That so," I said, and glared at Jack Terrence. A man's eyes can tell a lot about him if you look into them in the right instant. It only took a moment to size up the truth about Jack Terrence, and I thought I had it down pretty good. It was a gamble, but I was betting my life that the big bag of wind before me was nothing more than that, a bag of wind who liked having the upper hand and pushed it for everything he could get. But a killer? No.

"A big time Dan'l Boone, huh?" I said, continuing to stare at him in my own mad way. "Tell me something, Terrence, are you used to seeing a man's guts falling out in front of you? Can you put a slug in a man and walk away without puking? Are you man enough to kill another human and sleep the night through without having it on your mind? I've seen men who call themselves man killers." I yanked a thumb over my shoulder. "Ben there, now he's a man killer."

At the sound of my words, Ben brought his rifle to his shoulder and took a bead on Jack Terrence. "Damn straight, mister," I heard him say.

"You may be a tough hombre, Terrence, and you can shoot, I'll give you that." I shook my head as I said, "But you ain't no killer."

Quartermain suddenly brought up the Spencer in his arms and leveled it at Jack Terrence's back. It caught Terrence off guard, for I don't believe he was expecting it. Not at all.

"I don't know the truth of what he says, Jack,"

117

Quartermain said, his voice a mite shaky. "But if the man'll speak good for me, by God, I want him alive when we get back. I'd appreciate it if you'd put that rifle down and give us all a chance."

I caught myself wondering why in hell Quartermain would be willing to go back with us when he had the drop on us, but like I say, you can tell a lot from a man's eyes. Quartermain gave a nervous look past me and it crossed my mind that what I'd said about Ben being a man killer might have made the man think. But I was wrong. Glancing over my shoulder I saw that Pa had taken a bead on Quartermain with his own rifle. Like it or not, the man had set a course for survival.

As for Jack Terrence, he had more than a little sweat coming down his forehead now, as he did some heavy thinking. When he was through, he put the rifle down.

CHAPTER

★ 13 ★

I sent Pa and Ben after the horses, while Wash, me, and Terrence and his cohorts dug a shallow grave for Handy. I reckon you could say that Handy had lived up to his name, for he had come in right handy at the end of that Indian raid. But I wasn't thinking much about the humorous side of things just then. Hell, it was a downright shame to see the man die. That was something else I'd come away from the war with, a hatred of death. Still, it seemed to surround me, which didn't make accepting it any the easier.

Actually, it was me and the Terrence group who dug the grave. I had Wash keep an eye out for any more intruders who might have revenge on their minds after our little set-to. But nothing came of it and we pretty much had the man planted by the time the sun was fixing to leave us for the day.

It surprised me that I didn't get any more trouble from Jack Terrence. He spent the afternoon helping out as much as he could and doing his part. Had I broken his spirit? Or had I uncovered him to his friends as a fraud? Both were possible, although I easily discounted both. Despite being a bag of wind at times, Jack Terrence was impressing me as too big a man with too much spirit to be broken that easily. But what bothered me most was the nagging question in the back of my mind. What was it I knew about him that I couldn't put my finger on? I hoped it would come to me soon.

When we caught up with Pa and Ben, they had rounded up the horses, which hadn't been much of a job, according to them. The horses had run a couple of miles until they had come on a water hole that, although a mite shallow, was enough to give both the herd and our mounts enough cool liquid.

"Even got enough for coffee," Pa said when he finished telling us how his afternoon had gone.

"Good," was all I could say as I poured myself and the others a decent cup of the hot stuff.

Pa made supper while the rest of us were fairly quiet in camp. I reckon he knew that digging a grave was more than a casual chore for a man, for even if you only dig down a couple of feet, it is something that purely takes the starch out of a body. That's a fact.

"How long before you think the buzzards will get to him?" Jack Terrence asked after a while.

"Wolves will get him quicker than buzzards, ary they range this far out in this land," Garver said.

"We buried him a couple of feet down," I said. "Might be the next flash flood before they get to him."

"Too bad old Jose wasn't there to read over him," Ben added.

"Yeah, I reckon he deserved some sort of final words," Quartermain said.

The quiet that hung over the camp at supper that night was the kind that had a good deal of tension to it. Maybe it was a sort of reverence for the dead. Or maybe it was a lack of words on the part of all of us to say something proper about the whole day's events. Sometimes there just aren't any words for things like that. I was finding that out more and more as I aged in this land.

One thing I do recall about that night, and that was silently saying a few words over my food before eating my meal. Somehow it suddenly seemed proper, but not in front of a bunch of men. I reckon it was one of those things that was hard to explain too, if you know what I mean. It was something that your Mama brought you up to believe as being the right thing to do, but something that men hardly ever did together. I reckon it had something to do with manhood. Those may not have been the right words, friend, but they were the feelings I had, as uncomfortable as they might have been.

That night and the next day made up for whatever type of disturbance we had the previous day. It was quiet as could be. Hardly anyone talked that morning or at noon camp. By midafternoon I could smell water in the air and knew that we would be reaching a good body of water by the end of the day. It wasn't long before we came on the Rio Grande. But my gut feeling was there was more than just water in the air. It was danger that I felt would soon be upon us, and after the previous day's events, well, my system was ready to rebel at the notion.

"You feeling what I am, Wash?" I asked my brother as we came on the river.

"Yeah, a shiver ran down my spine not long ago. You reckon the remains of old Jefe's bunch is waiting for us?"

"Somebody's watching us, that's for sure," Pa said, riding up to us.

Ben rode up next, his rifle resting on his hip. Seeing him ride up like that confirmed what I'd told Terrence about Ben being a man killer if ever there was one. Men like him could sense death in the air and were quick to be ready for it.

"Looks like this is where we part ways, gents," he said with a smile. "I won't say it was all a pleasure, but I won't soon forget that Mexican woman's food. Right tasty, it was."

"Gonna be one of them soldiers of fortune, are you?" I asked.

He shrugged. "I'll head down Matamoras way and maybe join up with Shelby if he's still on the march."

"Don't want to join us on our trek back to Twin Rifles?" Pa said. "You'd be more than welcome."

"Ain't you forgetting something, Will?" Ben said with a sly smile.

Pa cocked a curious eye at him.

"I've got a notion that as soon as you cross the Rio,

why, you'll be taking that badge out of your pocket and pinning it on your shirt."

"Oh, yeah." Pa grinned. "Almost forgot the law's hunting you. Well, if that's the case, *vaya con Dios.*"

"You fellas better watch your topknot," Ben said. "You're gonna have to take care of yourselves now that I'll be gone. Could be a mighty hard chore, you know."

We all laughed at the man's words and told him to get the hell out of here. He bid us good-bye and turned to head back south aways.

No sooner had he left than I heard some movement to our east again. It was from this direction that Jefe and his group had come at us, that much I remembered. What I saw now was eight, maybe ten men riding in our direction.

"Pull that Spencer of mine out, Chance," Jack Terrence said as he rode up next to me. He had seen the men coming too. But what struck me as strange was the fact that he had called me by my first name. Maybe the man was changing after all. I pulled out the Spencer in his saddle boot, cocked it, and gingerly handed it to him.

"Don't do any shooting until I say so," I said.

They could have been a reinforced bunch of Jefe's cutthroats. Or they could have been some of the genuine force of Juarez's soldiers who were patrolling the border. As close as we were to the border, I didn't care which they turned out to be. As long as they didn't give me any grief about taking my horses back across the border, we'd be all right. But just in case they were less than cooperative, we all had our rifles out as the group approached.

"Buenas tardes," Pa said. I felt a shiver flow down my spine. Maybe it was because I remembered that the foofaraw with Jefe and his bunch had started the same way, with Pa speaking the same words. It was unsettling.

"I must know what your intentions are, senor, and why you are on the Mexican side of the Rio Grande," the leader said. I reckon he was trying to be as civil as he could; at least that was how his voice sounded. It was hard seeing what his face looked like, for he had his back a good bit to the sun and under that wide-brimmed sombrero he was wearing, well, it was hard telling if he was uglier than sin or one of those ladies' men you hear about.

"What I intend to do, mister, is take these horses across that river as soon as I get through with this palavering session," I said. I wasn't wearing any fancy sombrero, so I reckon he could see the less than friendly look on my face and the voice that matched it.

"Your horses?" the Mexican asked.

"That's right, mister," I said in a hard, even tone. *"My* horses. You know, everybody I've met in this land who's been on horseback has been ornery and unlikable, and I don't mind telling you that it's beginning to bother me. Now, if you don't mind, I'm gonna quit being neighborly and get this herd of mine back across the Rio and head on home."

"How do I know they are your horses, senor?" he asked. "I don't see a brand on them." Persistent cuss, he was.

"They're my horses because I say they are." I was

124

getting mad at this wide-hatted pilgrim. To Pa, I said, "You know, I ain't done this much explaining since Ma taught me letters."

"Look, amigo," Pa said, "these are his horses, just like the man said. They got stolen from his ranch 'bout forty miles north of here, and we tracked down the horses and the horse thieves." Pa nodded toward Jack Terrence, Garver, and Quartermain. "That's them right there."

Sombrero chuckled and ran off a rattle of words in his own language that got some guffaws from his men. When he finished laughing, he looked back at me and Pa. "But they are armed, senor. They do not look like prisoners to me."

"They're armed 'cause every man oughtta have a chance to defend himself, don't you think?" Wash said, throwing the same words I'd used on him up to them. It crossed my mind that he was picking up a few things after all.

"Mister, you head south a few miles and you'll find a bunch of yahoos who come on me just like you did," I said. "I don't rightly know who they are, or were, for that matter, but I can tell you that all but four of 'em are dead and being picked dry by buzzards and wolves."

"You didn't like them?"

"They pulled their guns and so did we. Conversation sort of dried up about then and a lot of lead poisoning went on. If you know what I mean."

Sombrero was fast with the six-gun he had in his waistband. I blinked my eyes and he had it drawn and pointed right at me. I wasn't sure what he had in mind, but it wasn't fun and games, of that I was sure. On the other hand, I didn't have to do much thinking about what I was going to do.

Ben did it for me.

About a hundred yards to the south a shot rang out about a second after Sombrero's fancy hat went flying off his head. The hat flew some into the air before dropping to the ground, while the bullet ricocheted off the water in the river and went off into parts unknown. The result was all of us looking to the south and the sound of the rifle report.

"Saved your ass again!" I heard Ben yell before whacking the barrel of his rifle across the rump of his mount, cussing something fierce in Spanish, and riding hell-for-leather south.

Sombrero was mad now, and pointing the pistol right at me, to boot. At the same time he was deciphering Ben's words which didn't speak well of Sombrero's mother.

"Hell, I didn't shoot you!" I said, which was the truth.

He ran some more words rapid-fire by his men and they did a left face and got in just as much a hurry to chase Ben as he had been to vacate the area.

Part of the reason they all but forgot about the horses and us was that, while they were distracted by Ben, we had all drawn our six-guns—Wash having both his Dance Brothers .44 and that funny-looking LeMat in his hands—and were pointing them all at arms length at the lot of them by the time they looked back at us. It was what you call a true Mexican standoff and since they figured that chasing one man

126

was a lot easier than making a fight with us, well, like I say, they turned tail and ran.

"Ain't that rudeness for you?" Jack Terrence said with a grin. "Didn't even say good-bye to us."

"I ain't gonna invite 'em back just for that," Pa said, watching them go.

"Let's get these cattle across the river before they do decide to come back," I said.

"Sounds good to me," Wash said and wheeled his horse toward the herd.

It surprised me that Jack Terrence didn't make another stand and try to get out of our grasp. It had almost been a ritual of sorts for him to try to escape. Instead, he and Garver and Quartermain gave me their Spencers. I let the hammer down real easy, placed them back in the boot, and moved out ahead of them toward the herd.

This time I didn't look back to see if they were still there when I crossed the river.

127

CHAPTER

★ 14 ★

That was about all the excitement we had, once we got back across the Rio Grande. It took a couple more days to get back up to Twin Rifles, but everything went fine, even with the prisoners. Hell, you'd have thought that Jack Terrence was some kind of model prisoner. Of course, Garver and Quartermain were watching him like a hawk too. I reckon saving their necks meant a mite more to them than it did to Jack Terrence, or so it seemed. I still had an uneasy feeling that Terrence might make a break for it, but the feeling subsided more and more with each passing day.

"What do you think they'll do to us, once we get back, Marshal?" Garver asked one night. Pa had pinned on his badge once we'd crossed the Rio, just like Ben had predicted, and it was hard for these men not to notice it.

"Well, the law frowns on horse thieves," Pa replied over after-supper coffee. "That's a fact."

"We got trees this side of the river, you know," I threw in, just as a reminder. "If I was real determined, I'd find me a good strong rope and stretch your necks." The thought of what these men had done to me purely riled me, and I reckon it showed in my words right then. I meant it and they knew it, and that was all that counted.

"Then how come you haven't done it yet?" Jack Terrence said, looking over his shoulder at me. I'd found out that when someone got mean with him, Jack Terrence got the same way with them. He didn't like my words or suggestions.

"I thought you had a brain, Terrence," Wash said.

"He's right, Jack," Garver said with a smile. "Whether you realize it or not, that Indian attack was the only thing that's saved our hides so far."

"That right?" Terrence growled. Like I said, he wasn't a real trusting soul at times.

"He's talking true to you, Terrence," Pa said. "I talked it over with the boys afterward and we agreed that ary you fellas behave yourselves, why, we might take to standing by you once we get back."

"How do I know I can trust you?" Terrence said.

"Tell me something, Terrence," I said, finding myself a mite put out with the man. Of course, that had never been hard to do with him. All you needed were the right circumstances, and a few words. "Didn't you southern boys place a lot of faith in a body's word?

That's all I've been hearing from my brother since we come back from the war," I said.

"Sure," Terrence said. "Shelby was always big on that."

"Well, I might have fought for the other side, but that don't mean I can't believe in the same thing." I pointed a hard finger at him. "Mister, you've got my *word* on getting proper credit for what you've done, good, bad, or otherwise." It didn't strike me until after I'd done it, but I suddenly gave a nod of finality, just like I'd seen Pa do so many times.

"And if Chance's word ain't enough for you, Terrence," Wash added, "you can count on mine. Hell, mister, I fought for Shelby too!"

"That's fine with me," Garver said.

"Me too," Quartermain agreed.

Jack Terrence grunted and turned his back toward us. I don't know if that was his way of snubbing us, or what, but I sure did feel like laying a boot to his butt. He was right trying at times like this.

"You boys seem to forget that I was a witness to all that you did during that Indian raid," Pa said. "Being a lawman, why, I got a notion that'll count for more than you think.

"Of course, when it's all said and done, I'd be wanting you boys to move on, just for the good of the community, you understand," he added, so they didn't get too confident of gaining their freedom. Me, I had my own way of letting them know that I wasn't putting up with any funny business.

"Now, there's a good strong cottonwood over yonder for you, Terrence," I said the next morning— pointing to one of the few trees in the area—when I rode up alongside the horse thief. I smiled at him and hefted the rope in my hand. "Of course, this rope is real strong too, you know."

"Is there a reason for that, Carston?" he asked after we stared at one another for a while.

"Just don't want you feeling too comfortable, Terrence, that's all." He got my message, so I left him alone from then on.

I was a day off in my prediction. It took us six days to get back to Twin Rifles, not seven. It was a welcome sight when we saw the makings of a ranch that Wash and I had started only a month or so ago.

"I don't see how you can ever make a go of it on a run-down place like this," Terrence said, smiling for the first time since I'd seen him.

"Watch your mouth, mister," Wash growled in as ornery a manner as Terrence was capable. But then, I couldn't blame him. Both he and I had put a lot of hard work into making this place stand for something. Having it degraded by the likes of Jack Terrence wasn't about to be tolerated. No sir.

"Wash," I said, trying to think quick before he decided to take on big Jack Terrence and get the hell beat out of him. "Why don't you take the horses and get 'em settled in, while Pa and me take these birds to town?"

"You're talking about a lot of work, Chance," he said with a lack of enthusiasm. "But I reckon someone's got to do it."

"Tell you what, brother," I said. "It ain't that much after noon. Once we get these fellas bedded down, I'll have Sarah Ann bring you out some fried chicken." I thought I saw Terrence flinch for a moment, but didn't pay much attention to him. "In the meantime," I said, jingling some of the double eagles still in my pocket, "I'm gonna square some accounts and get us set up with some feed for these horses. By God, we're gonna do it right this time."

The words heartened my brother, especially the words about Sarah Ann, and he smiled as he walked his horse toward the corral.

"Now you're talking," he said as we left.

The next stop was Twin Rifles. Just so folks wouldn't get the wrong idea about what was going on, we had Terrence, Garver, and Quartermain riding just a mite to our forefront while we rode into town on the left and right side of them.

I was on the left side, with Jack Terrence sitting stoically next to me. We came in from the south side of town, the same way we had left. I gave a yell for Sarah Ann when we got close to the Porter Café, figuring I'd put in my order for Wash's fried chicken. Hell, the whole town knew these two were sweet on one another, and I knew that I'd get that much more on my brother's better side for doing the favor.

"Oh, Chance, you came back!" she said, smiling.

"We Carstons always come back, Sarah Ann." I smiled right back at her. "Say, do me a favor, will you? Wash is tending the horses out at the ranch. He ain't et since sunup, and not too well at that. I was wondering if you could fix him some of that fried chicken of yours. I'll be back in about an hour and—"

I never did get to finish what I was saying. Sarah Ann turned the palest white I'd seen on a woman in a long time, let out a short scream as she looked at me, then began crying and ran back into the café.

Pa was leaning over the front of his horse, giving me the hardest look, as though he'd already judged me to be guilty.

"I didn't do anything!" I said, spreading my hands. "Nothing."

"That'll be the day," he said and urged his horse on. "Come on, boys."

"Everything's still in one piece," Joshua said with a smile as we pulled up in front of the marshal's office. Then something strange happened. He was taking in the prisoners when he came to Jack Terrence and his glance stopped for a moment. Then he shook his head and went inside. I'd bet a dollar the man was having the same thoughts I had about Terrence.

I looked Terrence over one more time and I knew I'd seen him before but couldn't place him. Maybe one of these days it would come to me.

We untied their ropes once we had them in the cells in back.

"That feels a helluva lot better," Terrence said, rubbing his wrists when he was free of the ropes.

"Joshua, I can use some of your coffee, if you've got any," I said out front.

"Did and done," he replied. I had to admit, if only to myself, that I had missed hearing him use his own version of the battered English language. When I had the cup of coffee in my hand, I appreciated it even more.

"Thanks, hoss, I appreciate it," I said.

"What the hell's going on!" I heard a deep bass voice spew from the doorway. Looking up I saw it was Big John Porter, Sarah Ann's father and owner of the Porter Café.

"What's the matter, John?" Pa said, puzzled. The man was obviously excited about something.

"Why, it's Sarah Ann!" he exclaimed. "She come in crying like someone had died and she won't tell me a thing."

"I was gonna ask about that," I said. "I leaned over and asked her to make some of that fried chicken of hers for Wash. He's out at the ranch with the horses we brought back." I shrugged. "She gave me a surprised look and busted out crying, just like you say. Don't it beat all?"

"You got all of 'em, did you, Will?" Joshua asked. "I seen three of 'em, but what happened to the fourth?"

"Handy was his name," I said. "Got himself killed playing a long shot. The big one, Jack Terrence, he figures himself for a tough one."

John Porter had been mulling over what to say next, what was wrong with his daughter, when he heard us talking.

"What did you say?" he asked. "Jack Terrence? That one of the men you brought in?"

"Yeah."

"Back there?" he asked, pointing a lengthy arm to the rear of the hallway.

"Yeah."

John Porter didn't ask permission to go back and see the prisoners, but then, Big John Porter did pretty much what he wanted to.

"You worthless son-of-a-bitch!" I heard him growl down the hallway. Then he came charging back up the hallway, looking as mean as Sarah Ann had been surprised.

"What is it?" Pa asked.

"That's Jack Terrence, all right," John Porter growled in anger. "Jack Terrence *Porter!* He's my son!"

Big John Porter stormed out of the room and back to his café. I reckon we all knew why Sarah Ann had been crying. Hell, I didn't even know she had a brother.

I glanced down the hallway at him, and it all fell into place. No wonder he looked so familiar! The shock of black hair, the mustache, and dark eyes. Jack Terrence was the spitting image of Big John Porter twenty-five years ago!

CHAPTER

★ 15 ★

He does tend to favor John, don't he?" Joshua said, making a statement more than asking a question.

"A lot, Joshua, a whole lot," I said.

"Almost reminds me of some of the foofaraws we've gotten into over the years," Pa said, breaking a smile. He was right, for I could remember days when my father had been less than hospitable toward me for what he deemed to be less than sane behavior. But that's a whole 'nother canyon.

Still, Pa and me had been able to patch up our differences over the years. John Porter and his son Jack were clearly at war with one another. It reminded me of the day I'd rode into town, the day I'd come back from the war. My brother had come in just a few minutes before me and was in the same saloon. Hell, the only saloon. We hadn't seen each other for a good four years, but as soon as I entered the saloon and saw the beat-up Johnny Reb uniform he was wearing, why, I reckon I went a mite wild. I'd gotten to hate Confederates so much that I automatically tore into him and did my damnedest to tear him apart. I hadn't even noticed that it was my brother until Pa came into the saloon and took on the both of us. Of course, that wasn't the first time that had been done either. If Jack Terrence hadn't been locked up, I had a notion he would have had the tar beat out of him by his pa.

I reckon I've been the most curious of the Carston Clan, and that curiosity was up now as I walked out the door of the marshal's office and headed for the Porter Café. I knew, for one thing, that Wash would never forgive me if I didn't get that fried chicken to him. Sarah Ann was waiting tables when I entered the café, but even from across the room I could see that her eyes were bloodshot from crying. I ducked back into the kitchen.

"I'll have your chicken ready for you in twenty minutes," John Porter said. Yes sir, he sure did look a lot like Jack Terrence. Hell, he even sounded like him. Or maybe it was the other way around. Depends on which direction you're riding on the trail, I reckon.

"Great," I said, "Wash will really appreciate it."

"Never seen a boy that could make fried chicken disappear as quick as Wash." He was trying to act like nothing had happened, like everything was all right. Me, I wasn't about to get on his bad side. I already knew what the result of that would be.

137

"Say, John, do you mind if I borrow your buckboard? I'm gonna have to get some feed out to the ranch, what with them horses being as underfed as they are."

"Sure," he said, without looking up. "It's out back."

"Thanks. I appreciate it. I'll be back for Sarah Ann and that chicken in half an hour or so."

His smile was forced as he said, "Yeah, I reckon she'll want to see Wash. She worries a lot about him."

"You noticed too, huh?" It was a sad attempt at humor that didn't come off the way it normally would, so I left it and John Porter be.

The folks at the feed and grain store were a little surprised that I not only paid off the existing bill but paid for my supplies in full and left the remaining money on account with them. It also made them quite happy to open an account with me. Believe me, I had no idea where I'd get money to pay off the outstanding balance when the bill came due, but it was nice for a change having people look at you with a smile. But then, I reckon money is the right thing to make you more acceptable to some folks, especially business folk in your community.

I loaded as much grain and feed as I thought John Porter's buckboard could carry without putting too much strain on the horses or breaking the buckboard all to pieces. It turned out to be a considerable amount. In half an hour I was ready to pick up Sarah Ann.

She gave me a feeble smile and got in the buckboard. I had tied my horse to the back of the buckboard, but she insisted on driving herself. "I need something to do," was all she said. So I rode my horse beside her as we left for our ranch.

We rode at a nice leisurely pace, although it may have been the heavy load that was slowing down the horses more than any lack of urgency Sarah Ann had about seeing Wash. We hadn't gone far when I saw she was crying. Silently, mind you, but crying all the same.

"Are those tears of happiness for seeing Wash or sorrow for seeing your brother?" I asked. I always figured you got from here to there by going in a straight line. That meant getting kind of bold at times, if you know what I mean.

"Both, I guess," she said. "I don't know."

"How long's it been since you seen him?"

She shrugged. "A long time. Ten, maybe fifteen years. I don't know." She gave me a forlorn look. "He just looked so much like Papa when you brought him in today. I never would have recognized him if it hadn't been for that."

"Did he give any signs of recognizing you?" I asked.

Again she shrugged. "Not that I could tell. Did he mention me?"

"Nope."

We rode a while longer as she regained her composure. The wind came up and shifted in my direction and I caught a whiff of the chicken she was carrying in a larger than normal picnic basket. It wouldn't be long before we'd be at the ranch.

"Your daddy wasn't too pleased to see Jack Terrence," I said after a while. "Think you'd know why? I sure don't."

"Like a lot of people, we got secondhand word of what Jack was doing during the war," she said. "Sometimes you don't know whether to believe it or not. But Papa did."

"Must've been pretty bad for him to cuss his own flesh and blood," I said, even more curious now.

"It was." I knew if I got pushy with her, she'd clam up tight, so I let her form her thoughts and then her words while she was silent. Her forlorn look had turned to true sadness and shame when she looked up at me and said, "Jack Terrence Porter was supposed to have fought with Quantrill's Raiders."

"That gang of cutthroats," I said, feeling the cords in my throat tense up as I spoke the words. Everyone knew about the murderous bastards who had been with William Clarke Quantrill and the legacy of death he had left in Lawrence, Kansas back in 1863. He and his men had burned the town to the ground, killing some one hundred and fifty men, women, and children in the process.

"That's exactly how Papa said it," she said.

"I can understand how he feels. Hell, if only a quarter of what I've heard about Quantrill is true, then I wouldn't blame him one bit for being angry."

The words hurt her, that much I could see. Her father was all but disowning her brother, and there didn't seem to be much she could do about the way he felt. It hurts something fierce to be put in between two relatives in a family fight. I know, I've been in that position myself. Still, I could see that it was hurting her more than it ever would me. It didn't seem right.

We were approaching the ranch when I said, "For

what it's worth, Sarah Ann, I don't think all the information you got was correct."

"What?"

"The first time we saw your brother, he was with a Confederate general by the name of Shelby, who was crossing the Rio Grande on his way to Mexico," I said. "Wash served with this Shelby fella and talks him up to be right up there with Robert E. Lee, and I know Lee and Shelby didn't fight anything like Quantrill.

"On the way back, your brother tried talking tough, apparently claiming to one of the men with him that he'd killed men. Trying to scare 'em or get their respect, I reckon. I called his bluff and I saw the look in his eyes." This time it was I who paused to put my words in the right order. When I spoke them, they were earnest, and I could only hope that this young girl would believe me. "Sarah Ann, your brother Jack is a flannelmouth and a hard case, and he likes the upper hand. But he ain't no cold-blooded killer, no matter what he or anyone else tells you."

For the first time since I'd come back that day, I saw Sarah Ann smile the way a pretty woman is supposed to smile. And when we neared the ranch, she was out of the buckboard and running into my brother's arms like he'd been away for a couple of years, not a couple of weeks.

But then, I reckon that's the way it should be.

CHAPTER

★ 16 ★

Don't be holding on to him too long, woman," I said to the couple as I dismounted.

"Huh?" both said at the same time.

I pointed to the buckboard. "Chicken's getting cold."

I've always thought that one of the reasons Wash was a mite skinnier than me was because I've always managed to grab the last couple of biscuits or piece of meat left on the plate at the supper table. Hell, there're times I've taken meat right off his plate when he wasn't looking and he didn't even know it. All it took was my mentioning food and the past came back to my brother's mind right quick like. Before I knew it he had snatched the basket of chicken and was hugging it as dear as he had Sarah Ann.

"Not this time, you don't!"

"War ain't done nothing to your memory, I see," I said with a smile. I sometimes think Wash tires of my ribbing him. But then, what's a little brother for if not to fun once in a while?

I knew there was coffee on the fire, so I got us some cups while Sarah Ann portioned out the fried chicken, along with some homemade biscuits. Naturally, she gave Wash more than me, but I wasn't complaining. It was the first home-cooked meal either of us had eaten since leaving Jose's adobe down south. I even found myself saying a silent prayer before I commenced to do away with the chicken in front of me. And you know something, hoss, I believe I saw my brother pause a minute before doing the same to his meal. I was glad we'd met Jose and his family.

Wash stopped a half-dozen times while eating, which must have felt unnatural. But each time it was to ask Sarah Ann or me a question. Sarah Ann was taking her time eating the small portion of chicken she had saved for herself, but then, she was telling my brother all about Jack Terrence and what had gone on in town. Me, I half listened to them while I savored the food and coffee. In fact, I had finished eating my meal while Wash still had half of his left. Sarah Ann had only taken a small bite of her chicken, but I had a notion the events of the day had soured her appetite some.

"You gonna be able to make it back to town without

an escort, Sarah Ann?" I said after wiping my hands and mouth off. I took one last swig of coffee and tossed the remains on the ground.

"I think so, Chance," she said with a smile. "Thanks for riding out with me. Talking helped some, and hearing your side of the story makes me feel a bit better about Jack."

"Good," I said and I was genuinely glad to hear her say those words. Life has a way of not being fair at all as you live through it, and getting help from your friends is about as close as you'll ever come to making it through in good spirits. Unless, of course, it's your family that gives you the help. That's the best kind you can have. Truth to tell, as much as I disagreed with my Pa and fought with my brother, I was feeling mighty glad to have them around. Yes sir.

"Before you head back to town, Sarah Ann, get him to promise you the recipe Pa picked up south of the border," I said. "Pa's gonna give it to Margaret and Rachel, so there ain't no reason you shouldn't have it too. Makes chicken real tasty."

"Chance Carston, are you saying—" she started with a frown.

"No, ma'am," I said, holding a hand up in defense. "Never. Maybe I should just say, this recipe will give your chicken a Mexican flavor." I mounted my horse. "Wash, I loaded that grain and feed. See if you can't find a proper place to store it."

"What're you doing?"

"Heading back to town. Maybe Kelly's Hardware can use some more rifles and pistols," I said. "I know we can sure use a few more dollars in the bank."

Wash didn't argue. I think he was enjoying the presence of Sarah Ann too much.

I took my time riding back to Twin Rifles. My horse had been pushed far enough on our trek to bring in the horse thieves and the horses, and by the time the sun set today I was going to give him a good rubdown and a decent feeding. But I also had some thinking to do and I took my time on the way back to town to do it.

It was hard to believe that a girl as nice as Sarah Ann could have a brother with a pure mean streak, like Jack Terrence. But that seemed to be the case. Still, after talking to Sarah Ann and taking into consideration what Terrence and his gang had done, both good and bad, it seemed worth discussing with Pa what kind of charges we should level against these fellows, or if we should bring any charges at all. I also found myself wondering if such thoughts weren't being brought about by the division I'd seen in the Porter family over Jack Terrence. Maybe they were.

Hell, when you got down to it, it wasn't one man who had explored or settled this country. It never would be. Not even George Washington or Tom Jefferson. No sir. I'd lived too long in this land not to know that it was families that would make the land. And after families, it was people working together. I found myself wondering if I wasn't getting soft, and knowing that to do so in the wrong instance would kill a man. On the other hand, a man could mistake compassion for being soft. Like I said, sometimes it all depends on where you've been on the trail, not to mention what you've seen and done. It all makes a difference. Or maybe I was remembering Jose and his wise words.

Maybe.

I was still mulling it over in my mind when I rode into Twin Rifles. But once I got past the city limits I was brought back to the present with the sound of loud noise and a disturbance coming from the marshal's office. At least that's what the group of men outside made it sound like.

At the least they were mad, although they weren't carrying any firearms that I could see. Still, I undid the thong on my Colt's .44 as I neared them. Joshua was standing outside the door, trying to calm them down. Or keep them from going inside, one.

"What's the problem?" I said, as I dismounted in front of the marshal's office.

"I think you'd better go inside, Chance," Joshua said above the noise. "This concerns you too."

Inside were the men of the town council, with Hubert Weatherby, the leader, doing all the talking. Weatherby was one of the only men I'd ever known who had ever worked up more sweat on his upper lip than under his armpits. The little beads of sweat on his forehead kept a handkerchief in constant view of one hand or the other. Of course, he stood about half a foot shorter and weighed fifty pounds more than me too.

"Will, this situation has gotten way out of hand," he said as I entered Pa's office.

"Practicing what you do best, are you, Hubert?" I said with a smile. Wash and Pa weren't the only ones I was pretty direct and sarcastic with. If I was disliked by some in town, it might well have been because I was a tad more than blunt with them. In Weatherby's case, I'd goaded him about being a self-righteous flannelmouth before. Rubbing it in never helped his disposition.

"You're the one to blame for this situation too, Chance Carston," he blurted.

"Do tell." I perk right up when people like Weatherby start blaming me for something.

"Well, what are you going to *do* about it!" he demanded, all but spitting on me.

"Not being able to read minds, the first thing I'm gonna do is find out what you're spouting off about," I said. Pa grinned and I knew that if Wash was there, he'd have busted out laughing. He didn't care for the Weatherbys of this world any more than I did.

"You watch your mouth, young man," Jason Wright said. "You're talking to the town council, and what we're discussing is the legality of what you, your pa, and your brother did. Word's gotten around about this little venture you Carstons went on and how you crossed the border to bring back John Porter's boy." Jason Wright was a long-time member of the town of Twin Rifles, just like Hubert Weatherby. Where Weatherby was stout and fat, Wright was of average height but a mite on the skinny side. A strong wind would blow him away. They had both seen better days.

"Mister Wright," I said, feeling the urge to cuss both of these men out, "I never did cotton to you. And you know why? People like you and Weatherby here are as big at being flannelmouths as John Porter's boy." I tossed a thumb in the direction of the hallway and Jack Terrence's cell. "I never liked flannelmouths at all. Not one bit. But there's a big difference between you two pilgrims and Terrence." The two town councilmen looked like they were about ready to bust. "Terrence has a better chance of backing up what he says than either of you two.

"Now, before you start running off at the mouth, mister, you might want to think what it was *you'd* have done if those were *your* horses that had gotten stolen," I said with a growl that had a touch of mean to it. "I told both Pa and my brother that I'd go to hell and gone to get those horses, if that's what it took!" I stuck a thick finger into Wright's chest, pushing him back a step. "You'd have done the same goddamn thing, so I'd watch what I was saying, if I were you."

"The boy's right," Pa said, a hard look coming to his face. "You fellas seem to have forgotten something. Wash and Chance were making a new start with that herd of horses they collected. You can't blame 'em for going off to all ends to get that herd back. Besides, you know as well as I do that anywhere south of here, why, the law ain't got no boundaries."

"It doesn't matter, Will," Weatherby said in a huff. "We're civilized people and the law has to be upheld." He gave a knowing nod, like he'd had the last word. But I wasn't in the mood for that. No sir.

"You know, fellas, Pa's a right good storyteller," I said. "I grew up learning the history of this country from his stories."

"What's that got to do with this situation?" Wright said.

"It's got plenty to do with this situation, gents," I said, going back to my mean and ugly look. "The stories I heard most were the ones about how Pa and Abel Ferris founded this town and fought tooth and nail to make a go of it. Didn't seem to matter what you had to do to make a go of it, back then, you just did it. Now, friend, you tell me how much difference there is in the start you folks made out here and what me and my brother are trying to do."

"There ain't any, Chance," Pa said, although it was Weatherby, Wright, and the rest of the town council he was glaring at when he said it and not me. "You raise a good point, son."

"Well, we'll see about that!" Weatherby said. "Damn it, Will, your authority stops at the Rio Grande. You could be in the process of losing your job." His eyes bulged as he said it, but I knew that Pa wasn't scared of him or anything he'd said. The Weatherbys of the world always resort to making threats when they can't answer the questions you pose to them.

"You can try hard as you want, Hubert," Pa said, "but it'll be a cold day in hell when that happens."

Weatherby and Wright didn't have an answer for that either, so they walked as hard and fast as they could to the door. I reckon it was supposed to be some kind of moral victory for them to do that. Politicians are like that.

"Don't let the door hit you in the ass on the way out," I said as they left.

"I don't know about Wright," Joshua said, "but it would be all but impossible for the door not to hit Mister Weatherby in the ass."

"Sometimes I think that's the only reason he ever wanted to get put on the town council, son," Pa said.

"Why's that?"

Pa smiled. "So he'd have some fart catcher to open and close doors for him."

I do believe Pa was right. I doubted that Hubert Weatherby was actually capable of doing something that simple all by himself.

Joshua, Pa, and me sat pretty quietly in his office for about an hour after the town council left. The most movement that took place was refilling our coffee cups, and Joshua making a new pot of coffee. Not even Terrence, Garver, or Quartermain made a noise. I reckon we were all wondering what to do next, for Weatherby and Wright were not without friends in town. I was half expecting a small mob to come knocking at the door before sundown. Instead, it was Wash who came through the door. He must've felt awful uncomfortable when he entered to be greeted by the three of us, each with his hand on the butt of his six-gun.

"Whoa, now," he said at the sight. To me he said, "I put that grain and feed away, honest, Chance." Then he breathed a mite easier when we left our pistols where they were and we told him what had happened since I'd returned that afternoon.

"Well, I'll be," he said. "Real uppity, ain't they?"

"What're you doing here?" I asked, suddenly concerned about losing the horses we'd just gotten back.

"I came back with Sarah Ann," he said. "Just wanted to see if this Jack Terrence looks anything like her pa." Without waiting for an answer, he sauntered down the hallway and took a long look at Jack Terrence. "Well, I'll be. He does."

Wash picked up a cup of coffee and joined us, but didn't seem content to mull anything over. Leave it to my little brother to be anxious.

"You figured out what you're gonna do yet?" he asked.

"I'm about ready to tar and feather the so-called town council," I said, still mad at the audacity of the men who'd threatened us.

Wash coughed and took a quick gulp of coffee, the way a nervous body will when they know that what they're fixing to say isn't going to be all that popular.

"Go ahead, Wash, spit it out," I said.

"Well, I was thinking, on the way in," he said in what can only be termed a shy manner. "What if we just let these yahoos go? I mean, they didn't really do us any harm. And they came in right handy when them Indians took us on. Sarah Ann would really like to see her brother, it being a long time and all. And—"

He never finished talking. As he'd said his piece, my

mind was whirling with emotions of my own. This was my brother speaking, my partner! Didn't he realize what we'd gone through to get those horses? Didn't he realize that he was my partner? Well, that tore it!

I dropped my coffee cup. At the same time I hit him with a straight left that sent him sprawling back. I followed it with a roundhouse right that flattened him, spilling his coffee. Then I stood over him and looked down on him, mean as hell.

"They stole our goddamn horses!" I yelled.

Like I said, my brother may be smaller than me, but he makes up for it with fast. By the time I'd gotten through speaking my piece he had recovered from my blows and was scrambling to his feet, a look of vengeance now on his face.

"Wait just a goddamn minute!" I heard Joshua say to my rear. He didn't normally speak that loud, and it was the first time I could remember hearing him yell as loud as I had. It brought Wash to a standstill as he looked over my shoulder in disbelief. When I was sure he wasn't going to hit me, I glanced over my shoulder too and discovered why he had the look on his face that he did. Hell, it wasn't what Joshua had said. It was the fact that he had his pistol out and pointed at the two of us!

"What the hell!" I heard myself saying in amazement.

"You boys want to bust each other up, you just step out front or out back," he said, "don't make no never mind to me." His voice still had the same drawl to it, but the look on his face was considerably harder than I'd ever seen it. "But you ain't gonna spill coffee on

153

my floor, boys. It may be summer, but winter's still a-coming and this here's a wood floor, and by God, I treasure my warmth in the winter."

"What're you talking about?" Wash said, as confused as me.

"What I'm talking about is how these floorboards is gonna shrivel up now that you've poured coffee on 'em, and let that much more cold air through 'em come winter. That's what I'm a-talking about!" His ire had grown with each word and he suddenly had a dangerous look about him. Behind him, Pa had the makings of a smile forming on his lips.

"Put the gun away, Joshua," Pa said, "although I can't blame you. He's got a good point, boys."

"What about these two?" the deputy asked, gun still in hand.

"They'll stop their fighting right now, or they'll have to fight me," Pa said, a determined look about him. "You remember what that's like, don't you, boys?" He smiled the way he did when he used to get ready to have us go out and pick the switch he was going to beat us with way back when. "I may be older than you two but it'll still take you a day and a half to get up off your ass when I get through with you." It wasn't a threat or a promise, like some men make. It was fair warning. That was how Pa operated. And yes, we did remember.

"You've been acting awful mean, Chance," Joshua said, holstering his six-gun, "especially since those horses got stole from you."

"I like to call it determined," I said.

"Obsessed would be more like it," Wash said,

although he made sure he was a good six feet away from me when he said it.

"The boy's right, son," Pa said. "I stood by you when you crossed the Rio Grande because you're my son and I know that you've been through a war and you're starting over, just like I told the town council. But the truth of the matter is that ary I'm gonna go up against the town council and maybe the people of this town, I'd like to know a little more of the *why* I'm doing it. I'm sure you've got your reasons, Chance. I just think you owe us the knowing of what they are. It'll make it considerably easier for us when the time comes."

I was silent for a few moments, mulling over in my mind what Pa had said. It was true all right. I had been as mean as a rattlesnake the whole trip down and back. Maybe the only soft spot I'd let show was meeting Jose and his family. Otherwise, I'd been pretty curt with just about everyone. No denying it. I reckon Pa was right. I did owe them a reason for what they were about to get into with the town council.

"I never did tell you where I was or what I did during the war, did I?" I said. Wash had let slip bits and pieces about where he'd been and who he had been with, like the stories about Jo Shelby after we'd met up with the Confederate general a couple of weeks back. But I'd kept quiet about my war experiences. My cavalry hat was the only indication of what I might have done.

"I always figured that you'd talk about it whenever you got ready to," Pa said.

"Well, I reckon war does change a man some," I said, pouring more coffee all around. "Joshua, why don't you put on another pot of coffee and I'll tell you all a story."

And that I did.

Like a lot of soldiers on both sides of the war, I'd been a lot of places and done a lot of things. Some were forgettable, while others a man would never forget. The story I told them was burned in my memory forever.

They called it the Red River Campaign and it lasted from February 29 to April 27 of 1864. Almost two months. It was a bastard.

I was serving under the Union General Nathanial P. Banks at the time, which didn't impress many of us, since the man wasn't one of the more competent generals our army had. With a combined force of naval and military weapons and men, we were supposed to move against the Shreveport Confederate headquarters and disrupt the Johnny Reb movement in Louisiana.

But the whole thing turned out to be one of the biggest fiascos I'd ever been a part of in my life. The so-called campaign took all of seven weeks and we did our share of fighting against the Confederates, that's a fact. But the rapids on the Red River all of those naval gunboats were supposed to come up and give us support from, never got any higher than three feet! And when they dammed it up so it reached seven feet, why, those gunboats were as useless as could be, getting potshotted at from the banks on the Confederate side so bad that they were useless as buffalo chips in one of those fancy back east salads. But that wasn't the worst of it, not by a long shot!

It got worse when a good portion of the troops U.S. Grant had committed to the campaign got called back by Grant himself. Turned out later he needed them for that Atlanta Campaign Sherman took all the credit for. By that time, most of us figured they had flatforgotten about us. The way it turned out, I reckon they did.

That was the worst part. Those Johnny Rebs were some brave lads. I can swear to it because I fought some of them, and they never stopped coming until they'd drawn that last breath. But we outfought them at least ten-to-one!

"Think about that," I said, "killing ten Rebs for every one Union soldier killed. Just think about it a minute."

"Sounds fearsome brave, Chance," Wash said. "I'll give you that."

"You had to be there to realize that it was just plain stupid," I said, the red creeping up my neck. I could almost cry remembering the futility of those shooting matches.

"Sounds like you won," Pa said.

"Not hardly!" I took one last gulp of my cup of coffee and told them the sad truth. "After we won, we *retreated* from the very ground we had taken."

"You're joshing me!" Wash said in disbelief. "That don't make no sense!"

"No sense a-tall," Joshua said, scratching his head.

"Well, like I said, General Banks wasn't the kind of soldier who ever impressed the men who served under him. He was long on command and short on guts."

I poured another cup of coffee before throwing in the kicker I knew they were waiting for. I was hoping they heard every word too, for I had no intention of retelling this story ever again. It embarrassed me that much.

"After fighting that hard for something we never even kept," I said, "I swore that I'd never be the subject of that kind of injustice again. I reckon you could say that the Rio Grande was just one more river that hadn't hit high water, just like the Red River, and I was damned if I was gonna let it stop me from getting back my horses.

"And that's that." I shrugged. "Take it or leave it, that's why I went back after them horses the way I did."

"I can understand it, Chance," Pa said. "I do believe I'd have done the same thing."

"First time I ever heard you speak well of a Confederate," Wash said. "There may be hope for you yet," he added with a smile.

"My watch tells me Miss Margaret ought to be about to serve the evening meal," Pa said, glancing at his pocket watch. "You boys care to join me? I'll bring you something back, Joshua."

"That'd be just fine," the deputy said.

Pa and Wash had already gone and I was about to leave when Joshua gently took hold of my arm. His voice was back down to soft when he spoke.

"You must've been a right fine soldier, Chance," he said.

"Why's that?"

"Why, I'd have shot that low-down general to smithereens," Joshua said in mock anger. "Hung him too, ary they'd had the time."

I smiled. "Believe me, hoss, when that campaign was over, we were about to draw straws."

CHAPTER

★ 18 ★

Most of Margaret Ferris's customers were already being fed by the time we reached the Ferris House. They were eating and talking at the far end of the community table and I had a notion Pa was going to want to discuss our predicament, so I put my git-up-end down on the side nearest us as we entered the dining area. I figured it would give us a bit of privacy. Margaret and Rachel were all smiles, but then, they were that way to just about everyone they met.

"You just missed some of the town council," Margaret said.

"Must've been Weatherby," Pa said with a smile. "I don't believe he's missed a meal in twenty years."

"It's just as well, if you ask me, Mama," Rachel said. "I think there'd have been a fight if they and the Carstons had met."

We settled on a steak apiece with home fried potatoes and biscuits. I told Margaret to burn the meat until it was well-done, figuring we'd have some time to talk before we ate. Rachel had coffee on the table before her mother was through taking our order. When she poured mine, she said, "I'm glad you made it back all right."

I smiled at her. "Fella we rode out of here with said he knew we'd be coming back as soon as he saw how pretty you women were. I reckon he was right."

Rachel blushed as she hurried back to the kitchen area.

"Well, what do you think, Pa?" I said when the women were out of sight. "You got any ideas on how to handle the city council?"

"I don't know, son," he said, a worried look on his face. "Weatherby and Wright seemed pretty upset about the whole thing. Acted like they were hell-bent on getting things done their way too."

"You know better than to let those flannelmouths try and push you around, Pa," I said. "Hell, you and Abel Ferris founded this town. That ought to count for something."

"Don't seem to make one whole hell of a lot of difference to me," Wash said. All of a sudden he had our attention.

"How's that?" I asked.

"Well, it seems to me that when we three were rangers before the war and we had to chase someone, no boundary and river ever stopped us in getting 'em," he said. "Did it?"

"No, it didn't," Pa said. "You've got a real good memory, boy."

"As I recall, folks around here were right grateful for our services back then too," Wash added.

Wash was right. I could remember the years before the war when the three of us had chased everything from Comanche to desperadoes all over the state of Texas, and that included horse thieves. Hell, anyone who had a long rope was subject to getting a stretched neck if they didn't find a new home and a new profession real quick. I reckon you could say it was sort of the unwritten law.

Wash had been right about folks being grateful for what we did too. Like I said, I wasn't all that well liked hereabouts in my youth, but I did have a good deal of respect for my ability to function as a Texas Ranger. Thinking back on it made me chuckle to myself.

"What's so funny?" Pa asked.

"I was just thinking over what Wash said," I said. "Seems this town has all of a sudden got a case of righteousness about right and wrong. Of course, it doesn't directly concern them, so I reckon they figure they can be as high and mighty as they like."

"Could be," Pa said.

"I wonder if maybe it ain't the war," my brother said. You didn't often see Wash in a thoughtful mood, but he sure was hitting the right thoughts tonight.

"How's that?"

"Well, Texas was a part of the Confederacy," he said, "no matter what Chance thinks." He shrugged. "You know, I've been too busy since I come back to do much thinking on it, but I reckon being on the losing side of a war doesn't set well with anyone. Folks who didn't fight it get about as ashamed of their menfolks as they do about being on the losing side. I don't mind telling you that it's got me to thinking."

"I know what you mean," Pa said, thinking back. "It was near the same way with that Mexican War." He shook his head in disbelief. "Seems like, when it was all over and done with, the only folks who really took a liking to what we did was the fighting men themselves. I reckon that's why I stayed out here." He chuckled to himself. "Hell, we wound up getting more sympathy from the people we was fighting out here than we would have from those fools back east."

Wash and I laughed with him and agreed. When you got right down to it, the Mexican people who originally lived in Texas before the War for Independence back in '36, were a friendly lot if ever there was one. They just wound up getting fired up and fighting on the wrong side half the time. I knew without asking that Wash would agree with that, for he'd done the same thing himself. It made me wonder, briefly, where this Juarez character would lead the Mexican people now that he was their hero.

Our food came and it was good. All you had to do was look at those steaming plates of steak and biscuits to know it was good. But it was better to eat it and find out again that you were eating some of the best food this part of Texas had to offer. I was cutting my meat up when Pa dug his hand into his pocket.

"Here you go, Margaret," he said, handing her a slip of paper. "A family we visited south of the border had some delicious chicken they fixed for us. I convinced the young lady doing the cooking to give me her recipe. Told her I was giving it to the best cook in the state." He winked at her.

"Careful, Will," Margaret said, kissing Pa gently on the forehead and smiling. "You're flirting again." She quickly snatched the paper from Pa's hand and read it on the way back to the kitchen.

It took me all of fifteen minutes to finish off my meal and a couple more cups of coffee, but I found myself doing some thinking too. Maybe it was because the situation, although not desperate, was beginning to stick in my craw and had my full attention.

"You set a fine table, like always, ladies," Pa said when he was through, just a few minutes after me. Both Margaret and her daughter were out there, taking our plates and pouring one more cup of coffee for all of us.

"You think any better about what your brother said earlier?" Pa asked me as he sipped his coffee.

"What's that?"

"The prospect of letting these yahoos go without charging 'em with anything. Part of what he said makes sense, especially if you consider that they helped us out when we needed it the most."

"It still rankles me that they'd steal the horses and then get off," I said with a frown. "Hell, for all I know they could up and steal 'em again. And I don't mind telling you, Pa, that as much as I liked Rosa's cooking, I'm not all that crazy to have another helping of it after I've chased horse thieves again."

"I could read to 'em from the book," Pa suggested. "Let 'em know that ary I saw 'em again in this area, why, I'd make dead meat out of 'em, no questions

164

asked." He scratched the back of his head in thought. "Of course, I don't know how well John Porter would take that."

"Don't worry about Big John," Wash said. "The way he's acting now, he couldn't care less whether Jack Terrence dies or not. It's Sarah Ann who's gonna come after you with Big John's horse pistol, Pa. I know what she thinks of her brother. Why, I'd practically guarantee it!"

Pa pulled out his pocket watch and glanced at the time. He rose to his feet as he said, "Be that as it may, I'll face it tomorrow. Maybe Weatherby and his crowd will have calmed down a good bit and we can talk some sense into them."

"Could be," I said, "but I ain't counting on it."

"See you tomorrow, Pa," Wash said and pulled one of the gold pieces we'd taken off of Jefe's bunch of toughs as payment before slapping on his hat.

I put my hat on too and left, thinking that for a gold piece like the one my brother had laid down, we should be getting our next week's worth of meals for nothing. Twenty dollars could go a hell of a long way.

CHAPTER

★ 19 ★

The next morning I told Wash I was going into town after we'd had breakfast. I reckon younger brothers don't take to being told what to do.

"You sure are acting like you own this place instead of being a partner in it," Wash said at the table. The inside of our ranch house isn't anything to brag about but it'll do for a couple of men living the bachelor life. Besides, everyone knows things don't start looking pretty or like they belong until a woman puts her touch to it.

"Hell, somebody's got to be responsible around here," I said. My brother tried cocking a questioning eye at me the way Pa does at times, but it didn't look right on him. "The way you've been looking at Sarah Ann, I'm surprised your brain is working at all."

Wash blushed and didn't say any more.

"You find some more deadwood if you can this morning and I'll come back this afternoon and split it for firewood," I said, drinking the last of my coffee. I put my hat on, then strapped on my gun belt and was checking my Colt's when I added, "You come into town about noon and you can spend the afternoon ogling Sarah Ann, if you like."

"What're you gonna be doing?"

"I dropped those guns off at Kelly's Hardware yesterday," I said. "Kelly's gonna take a look at 'em and give me a price this morning. We still gotta put some money in that bank, you know."

Wash grumbled and finished his own meal. He was out and about when I left for town.

Small towns take it easy waking up most of the time. But when I rode into town that morning I noticed a bit of tension in the air. I also took note that the few people who were on the streets noticed me as I rode into town. All of a sudden, I had the feeling I was the subject of conversations I didn't know anything about. It gave me a restless feeling, not to mention a suspicious one, and I undid the thong on the hammer of my pistol after I dismounted.

"What's going on?" I asked Kelly as I entered his store.

"Weatherby didn't waste any time getting the people stirred up again this morning." He shook his head. "I'd bet a dollar the first person he told was the town gossip."

"That was probably the only person he told," I said.

EX-RANGERS

We both walked to the back of his hardware store, knowing good and well the subject would be the rifles and pistols I'd brought in the previous day, which was why I had returned. Kelly had the weapons laid out on a table near the gun rack he kept in the rear.

"I cleaned 'em and checked 'em out," he said. There were seven rifles of varying sorts and nine pistols, all looking brand spanking new. Kelly knew his guns and did a good job on them.

"I was figuring on asking a couple hundred for the lot of 'em," I said. Kelly looked taken aback. "Don't you think that's an honest offer?"

"In a big city it might be," he said plain and simple. "But the economy's bad enough after the war and all, and this ain't a big city." I understood what he meant. Suddenly, the war being over was having one helacious effect on the economy just about everywhere.

"What was you fixing to give me?"

He shrugged, as though pulling a figure out of thin air. I knew better than that. "A hundred dollars."

"What!" I said, likely waking up those who weren't already. "You know good and well those are worth every bit of two hundred dollars! Look, I'll come down to one seventy-five. How's that?"

"I can only give you a hundred. It's all the cash I can spare right now."

It wasn't that Kelly was trying to cheat me or anything, for I knew him to be an honest man. But I was damned if I was going to let all these firearms go for only a hundred dollars.

"Tell you what, Kelly," I said, scratching my jaw as though it would make the thinking process easier, "I'll take a hundred in cash now and seventy-five on my

168

account with you." I paused a moment and added, "My brother and me make shirts last a long time. Hell, we was in the war." That was just about the truth too, for I could remember days when I thought my uniform could walk by its own self when I traded it in for a fresh one. But then, I reckon that's one of the joys of war, learning to appreciate what little you have when you have it.

This time it was Kelly who did the thinking, giving me a scrutinous eye as he did.

"No," he said. "One hundred cash and fifty dollars credit on your account."

"Done," I said and offered my hand before he changed his mind. It wasn't as much as I'd hoped for, but it sure beat having nothing all to hell. I had stuck the wad of money in my pocket and was about to leave the store when Weatherby and Wright entered. It was plain to see they weren't here to be looking the store over.

"There you are, Carston," Weatherby said. "I want to know what you're going to do about those men in jail."

"Then hadn't you ought to be asking me?" Pa said from behind them. I knew he was fed up with these town councilmen and the way they'd been spouting off, especially Weatherby, and it showed by the look on his face and the cold, hard as stone sound of his voice. "I'm the law, you know," he added, just in case they had forgotten.

"Your days may be limited, *Marshal,*" Wright said, although even trying to sound as tough as Weatherby was a chore for the skinny man.

"Oh, shut up, Jason," Pa said. "If you recall, I'm the

only one in this town who had the experience or desire to take the job of lawman after the war started and our boys all left for it. I doubt you'll get much backing from the folks in this town on that matter."

"I was wondering what the status was of the men in jail," Weatherby said in a calmer tone. As blustery as he could get, he was still one of the few men on the town council who had a bit of tact about him. "Are you going to release them? Have they been released yet?"

"No, they haven't, and I've been thinking about it," Pa said.

"You gonna turn 'em loose?" I asked, feeling my blood start to boil again.

"Now, just wait a minute, Chance," Pa said, holding a hand up for quiet. "Let me explain this thing. I've been thinking on it, and what Wash said sounds like it might bear out. They did give us a whale of a lot of help fighting off them Kickapoos. Why, you were there, son, you seen it with your own eyes."

What Pa had said was true. Jack Terrence, Garver, Quartermain, and especially Handy, had all shown they had the fighting spirit that day with the Kickapoo. No doubt about it, we would all be dead men if they hadn't pitched in to help us out. Still . . .

"I don't know, Pa, it don't seem right." I suddenly found myself wondering if I shouldn't have thrown a rope over that cottonwood I'd shown Jack Terrence that day and just be done with all three of them. It seemed like it would have saved everyone a whole lot of grief.

"You have to let them go!" It was Weatherby again, his tact turned to excitement. "It's against the law!"

"Is it election year, or are you just trying to see if you can throw your weight around?" Pa asked the fat man. "Lord knows you've got enough trouble *carrying* it around.

"You know, Weatherby," Pa continued, taking a step closer to the fat man as he poked a finger in his chest, "you're getting to be a burr under my saddle that I'm about to pick off and throw as far as I can." The thought of physical violence didn't set well with the fat man, who had turned a mite green around the gills. "Now, you and your town council had better hear one thing, loud and clear, my friend. If I turn any of those yahoos loose, it *won't* be from any prodding you two have done. It'll be because I've made the decision myself. Understand?"

"Y-y-y-es," Weatherby stuttered, fear in his eyes.

"Looks like company, Pa," I said, catching sight of a group of men pulling up in front of the store. Since we were right near the entrance, we all stepped out on the boardwalk. Pa squinted as he looked over the man who seemed to be the leader.

"You're just the man I want to see," the man said with a confident smile.

"That a fact," Pa said. "Well, speak your piece."

"You can call me Vegas," he said, still smiling.

"Name don't matter much at this point," I said in a blunt manner. I was also glad I'd undone the thong on my holster.

"Now then, what was it you said was on your mind?" Pa said.

"Why, I've come to take your prisoners." His smile reminded me of a sly cardsharp I'd seen once. They always thought they could outguess you. Most of them wound up finding a new line of work, for they didn't pan out as gamblers.

"It'll be a cold day in hell, mister," I said, my hand suddenly balling up into a fist.

"Not while I'm marshal, you won't," Pa said. I heard Pa pulling his Remington, and followed suit, both of us showing our hardware in a flash. The man who called himself Vegas held his hands up, palms facing us, still smiling confidently.

"Whoa, now, Marshal," he said. "I'm not pulling any guns on you. I aim to do this all peaceful like."

Hubert Weatherby suddenly got over being scared to death and spoke up. "Marshal, you said you were thinking about letting them go, remember?"

Pa's glance at Vegas and the men surrounding him was a hard one. He looked my way to see that I was watching this motley crew of riders before he turned his attention to Weatherby.

"Weatherby, I'm getting awful goddamn tired of people trying to tell me what to do in this town," he said in a forceful manner. "Now, until you find yourself pinning on this badge, I'd appreciate it if you just kept your mouth shut."

Weatherby looked as though he had been backhanded, which didn't seem like a bad idea to me. It would likely sober the man up a good deal. But Pa was ignoring him now, turning his attention back to Vegas.

"Somehow, you just don't strike me as the magistrate type, 'cause that's all that's gonna get those boys out of my jail," Pa said.

"You said you came to get those boys out of jail?" Weatherby asked in amazement. Then he smiled, knowing that he had someone who agreed with him. "Well, now—"

"Just who the hell are you?" Pa asked, a scowl coming to his face. "And why are you here?"

Vegas smiled a crooked smile. "Just like I said, Marshal. My name is Vegas, and I come to get those boys out of jail."

Pa's look got harder, just like his voice. "Well, you get that second notion out of your mind, mister. And make your stay in town short."

"And take your pack of wolves with you," I added.

CHAPTER

★ 20 ★

I crossed the street, heading toward the bank. But I'll tell you, hoss, I had a real uneasy feeling about turning my back on Vegas and his bunch. Calling them wolves wasn't far from wrong in my mind. Not after what I'd been through this past month.

Mind you, I'd seen my share of ragtag veterans returning from the war, most of whom were with Shelby and his men. But even with all the heroics my brother was telling me the man had performed in the war, I still found myself a mite sour on Confederates, for it was four of the men Shelby himself had recommended to me who had stolen my horses.

Then there had been the encounter with Jefe and his

wild bunch of no accounts. They hadn't impressed me much except for the killing look they had about them. As I recalled, they didn't last long either. The Plug Ugly that Jose, Pa, and I had buried, hadn't been much different. If anything, it was he Vegas reminded me of. I looked over my shoulder twice before I got to the other side of the street.

As for Indians, well, hoss, they were a lot like Mother Nature and the very land itself out here. They would likely be with you the rest of your life. It was just that sometimes you got along real fine with them and sometimes you didn't.

I was pulling the wad of money Kelly had paid me out of my pocket in front of the bank, when I saw Vegas follow Pa across the street. The bank was only about three buildings down from Pa's office, so it wasn't hard to overhear their conversation.

"It's easy to hear gossip in this town, Marshal," Vegas said. "Especially from that very plump little woman who was jabbering away at the edge of town as we rode in."

Pa nodded. "Yeah, that's Lucy all right. The town will likely just shrivel up when she dies away."

"You're right about my not being a magistrate," he said with that devilish smile again. "But I did study law before the war and I do know the ramifications of the law."

"Well, bully for you, son," Pa said. I had a notion he didn't like that smile any better than I did.

"And if what I hear around town is true, why, you have no choice but to let those men go," Vegas said. "It's as simple as that." You'd think he had everything wrapped up just the way he wanted it. I don't know if he was making Pa worry so much as he was making him mad. But then, he hadn't tangled with Pa yet either.

"I'm afraid it's not that simple, mister," Pa said in his best stern manner. "I just got through explaining that to our town council. But I'll take care of it, that's my job."

"But, I don't understand—"

"Mister Vegas, you don't strike me as the kind who does understand, although I'd swear you were speaking the same language as me," Pa said, good and mad now. "Mind you, now, there're times when the law has to be bent a mite. I'll give you that. But mister, I'll be the one who decides when to bend it and when not to. Now, you take those pilgrims that come with you and get you a drink and move on out of here right quick. Understand?" By the time Pa finished talking his voice had raised high enough for everyone within sight to hear him real well.

"All right, you've made your point," Vegas said. "I was just wanting to cut the dust anyway."

"Then do it and be quick about it," Pa said. He was about to turn away from the man when he stopped and said, "By the way, mister, just what kind of an interest do you have in those four men in my jail, anyway?"

I could tell by the shrug he gave that Vegas wasn't wanting to explain any more than he already had to Pa. "Just professional interest. That's all."

Whatever "professional interest" meant, it would be for Pa to figure out, for Vegas quickly headed back across the street to the saloon and his men. I made a point of counting the men who had come with him. At first glance, I thought I'd seen at least half a dozen or so. I was right about the half dozen. The "or so" turned out to be three more, making a total of ten men, if you counted Vegas. They weren't too shabbily armed either, from what I saw at a quick glance. Three carried rifles while the rest had at least a pistol and a bowie knife, sometimes two pistols on their body, along with what could have been an extra one on the saddle. They weren't peaceful men, of that I was sure.

Abigail Cross was the loan teller at the bank. She was probably in her forties and had snow-white hair. She was also one of the kindest women I had ever met. Wash had been right about how some folks looked at you with a certain amount of shame when you came back from the war. I had seen that in a good many of the residents of Twin Rifles. But not in Abigail Cross. She had helped me get an account started when I'd come back from the war a couple of months ago, and had done it cheerfully, even when twenty-five dollars was all I had to deposit.

"Morning, Miss Abigail," I said, taking my hat off while I counted my money out to her.

"Good morning, Chance." She looked past me, as though seeing something out the window. "I thought I heard your father out front."

I smiled. "He wasn't directly out front, ma'am, but you likely heard him all right. Strangers rode into town that don't look none too friendly, you ask me. I figure Pa's feeling the same about it." Anyone else might have balked at the thought, but Abigail Cross was about as friendly as the Ferris women on a full-time basis. Today she seemed right chipper and I said as much.

"How are you at keeping a secret, young man?" she asked me carefully. She had lowered her voice, although I don't know why, for there wasn't anyone else in the bank but the manager in his office.

"As good as anyone, I reckon. Why?"

"Well, Jason Wright's been seeing me for some time now, you know," she whispered.

"No, ma'am, I didn't." I wasn't going to insult her by reminding her that there had been a war going on for the past four years of my life, and the news of what went on in Twin Rifles had been farthest from my mind. All I remembered was that her husband had died before the war. But like I said, I liked Miss Abigail.

"Well, Jason asked me to marry him!" she said in a voice that wasn't quite a whisper anymore. The fact of the matter was, she was about ready to bust with excitement. "Isn't it wonderful?" she added with one of the widest smiles I'd ever seen on her face.

"Yes, it is, ma'am," I said softly. "I'm happy for you. Mighty happy."

Then her smile was gone and she looked at me in a quizzical way. "Strange," she said, "I never thought I'd hear you speak words like those or say them so softly."

I shrugged, not certain how to react. "Seems I've been surprising a lot of people of late," was all I could think to say.

She was quiet while completing my transaction, speaking to me only after I'd thanked her and put my hat back on, readying to leave.

"Chance."

"Yes, ma'am," I said over my shoulder.

"It's hard to avoid hearing gossip in this small a town," she said. "You stand tall and stick to your beliefs. It's the only way you'll ever amount to anything in this land."

"Yes, ma'am," I said. "I'll do just that."

I couldn't help but wonder, as I left the bank, if Abigail Cross hadn't been a school teacher sometime or somewhere. But then, that wouldn't have been all that out of place, I reckon, for many a mother taught her children how to read and write in a land that was short on schoolhouses. I remembered my mother doing just that. At times like this, Abigail reminded me a lot of Ma. She surely did.

The horses were still in front of the saloon as I walked over to Pa's office. It was getting on toward high noon now. But eating time wasn't on my mind as much as Vegas and his men. I had a strange feeling, like I was being watched, all the way to Pa's office, which wasn't all that far but sure did seem like it that morning.

Joshua and Pa had their hands on the butts of their pistols as I walked in unannounced. They didn't take them away until they recognized me.

"I know how you feel," I said. "I got the same feeling walking over here."

Pa was over by the bars, apparently talking to Jack Terrence and his cohorts.

"Are you sure you don't know anyone called Vegas?" he asked. Terrence, Garver, and Quartermain all said no.

"Never rode with someone of his description?" Pa asked again. "Medium height, three-day growth of beard, devilish smile?"

Jack Terrence smiled. "You're talking about half the fighting men in the Confederacy. Hell, that's likely the same description of half the Union army, as well." He was right. War wasn't some fancy business where you got to shave every day and dress up like Weatherby and Wright. No sir. It was pure death and destruction, that's what war was. I'd wager that every man who served in that war had looked as raggedy as the description Pa had given. That's a fact. Remembering that made me think.

"I wonder if we've run into another bunch of rebs trying to make their way south to Maximilian?" I said, throwing in my own suggestion.

"They look armed well enough to be that," Joshua agreed.

"They're a puzzle, I'll say that," Pa said, running his hand over his jawline. With the beard he had it was sometimes hard telling if he had lice he was trying to get out of his whiskers or was genuinely thinking on something. But that was Pa, who could be a puzzle at times.

"How's that?" I asked.

"Well, if that Vegas feller knows half of what he claims, we could be in for a real start, ary he decides to join forces with our fearless town council."

"It doesn't make a helluva lot of sense," Joshua said. "If Terrence here don't know him, what in the devil does this Vegas character want with 'em?"

"I'm wondering what he meant by professional interest?" Pa added.

"I don't know, Pa," I said, "but I'm getting the idea more and more that not everyone who's coming home from this war is looking to find an honest job."

180

"You remember what I said about Ben, the first time I saw him and he rode out of town with us?" Pa said.

"That he'd run afoul of the law?"

"Yeah. Well, I've got the same feeling about this tough-looking bunch."

"War does its share of injustice to a body," Jack Terrence said. "If you were in it, you know what I mean."

Injustice. I'd used that same word when telling Pa and the others my story about the debacle that came to be known as the Red River Campaign. Yes, I knew what injustice meant. Hell, I'd experienced enough of it. It was why I had turned hard and mean in my quest to recapture my horse herd and the horse thieves who had taken them as well. Maybe there were other men who had fought in the war but who had lost their sense of fair play and decided that they had been denied a regular life because of the war. Perhaps that was injustice to them. Was it possible that by the end of the war, those same men had gotten so adept at killing, that they found death so impersonal that they thought nothing of doing in another human for the simple sake of looting his wallet? The more I considered it, the more it became a very real possibility.

I was looking out the window when I saw Wash ride into town. He pulled up alongside the horses of Vegas and his men, dismounted and went into the saloon.

"Pa, Wash just came into town," I said. "I reckon he got all of his work done, 'cause he's getting himself a drink."

A look of concern came over Pa as he pulled out his pocket watch and gave it a quick glance.

"They've had their hour's worth of drinking," he said, checking the loads of his Remington. "I reckon it's time to remind 'em of it." When he saw me checking my loads, he put a firm hand on my wrist. "You stay here and see ary you can't get some more information out of Terrence. I still want to know why those men are in town. Besides, if there's any help needed, I'm sure Wash can give me a hand."

So out he went, crossing the street and stopping at the bat wing doors of the saloon.

Suddenly, he had his hands high in the air!

And I was going for my gun.

CHAPTER

★ 21 ★

I ran out the door, gun in hand, ready to kill the sonsabitches! By the time I was on the boardwalk, Pa had disappeared inside the saloon and his figure was replaced by that of a man aiming a rifle dead at me. I ducked about the same time he pulled the trigger and a piece of wood went flying off the building to my rear. I couldn't tell you right where it hit, but it ricocheted off of something and bounced off my back. All I knew was it was too damn big to have been the bullet itself.

"Git in here, you damn fool!" Joshua said from the doorway.

I suddenly realized that it was useless for me to be out there if I didn't want to get killed. I had reservations about firing into the saloon because Pa and Wash were in it and I didn't want to be responsible for them getting killed. All I wanted at that moment was to get my brother and father out of the saloon. I also had a distinct desire to kill Vegas and as many of his men as I could get in my sights! Still, you had to be alive to do that, so I ducked back inside the marshal's office.

"What're you trying to do, get yourself killed?" Joshua said.

"If that's what it takes," I replied.

I looked out the barred window that fronted the jail and saw a half-dozen men running out of the saloon like quail flushed from a nest. If they hadn't been wearing town clothes, and if I hadn't identified the faces of some of them, I might have taken to shooting some of the town's citizenry. But I'd been in enough tight spots before to know that a cool head was a lot better than a fiery temper.

"Whoever Vegas and his men are, they've taken over the saloon, Joshua," I said.

"You ever figure out who they are?" Jack Terrence asked.

"That's what Pa was hoping you'd tell us," Joshua said without looking back.

"Give us some rifles and we'll help you get 'em back," I heard Garver say. "We helped you out with them Kickapoo. We can do it again."

"Damn sure betcha!" Quartermain said. I was beginning to wonder if the two weren't brothers or something, the way one talked up as soon as the other did.

"No thanks, boys," I said. "There ain't as many of 'em this time, and it ain't Indians we're dealing with."

184

Joshua opened the lock holding the rifles in their rack and grabbed a Henry, checking it for shells. "That's a fact," he said to the prisoners over his shoulder as he pulled a box of shells from the desk drawer. "Why, I done saw the faces of most of those fellers and they're so ugly their brains likely already dribbled outta their heads. If they's anyone with brains, it's that Vegas fella."

"What if they were born that way?" Jack Terrence asked.

Joshua had a dead serious look on his face when he looked at Terrence and replied, "Son, if I was that ugly when I was born, why, Mama would've drowned me in the river outta pure shame!"

Terrence smiled. "But you was born in the desert, right?"

I had a notion that if Jack Terrence hadn't been a prisoner, and we didn't have the current situation to deal with, Joshua would have taken the big man out on the streets of Twin Rifles and showed Big John Porter how to discipline his son.

"You fellas want to insult one another, wait until this fracas is over," I said, hoping they'd see that I was more concerned about my family than I was about who could talk the ugliest. There would be another time and place for that, and Joshua would likely find himself standing in line behind me before he could take on Jack Terrence.

"You wondering what I'm wondering?" Joshua asked, as he took his place by the window.

"That seems likely," I said. "I wonder what they're gonna do next?"

"Beats me," the deputy said. "But I'll tell you

something, Chance. If these fellers ran afoul of the law, like your daddy says, they sure ain't inviting your pa and brother to belly up to the bar in there."

In ten minutes we had our answer. I heard a thud against the door and opened it slowly to see a rock that had been pitched against it. A piece of string tied a note around it. I picked it up, half keeping an eye on the saloon, half expecting to get shot for my efforts. But no gunfire came and I was able to get back inside safely.

"What are they wanting?" Joshua asked, still watching the saloon.

"They'll let Wash and Pa go if we do the same with Jack Terrence and his men," I said after reading the scrawled pencil writing.

"Figures," Joshua said. "Looks like we got us a Mexican standoff."

"Are you sure you don't know these guys?" I asked Terrence. "'Cause they sure do act like they know you." It didn't make sense. But then, a lot of things had seemed that way of late. Like, why would you turn loose four men who stole your horses? At first glance it seems like a foolish question, but the answer was relatively easy once you took in the whole situation.

You turn them loose to get your brother and father back safe and sound. And that was that.

Still, there was the matter of giving in to a bunch of cutthroats just because they had the edge on you. It didn't sit right with me. I knew it didn't sit right with Pa and Wash either. That meant they were likely waiting for me to do something about it, and that meant there would be a lot of chance taking involved.

Joshua grabbed the key off the peg on the wall.

"What do you think you're doing?" I said.

"Letting these yahoos go," Joshua said. "Let 'em ride out of here, Chance. Let 'em go! Gitting your daddy and brother back alive is worth more than these pilgrims will ever amount to. You know that."

"There's more to it than that, Joshua," I said, taking the keys from his hand and placing them back on the wall peg. "I've got an idea of what kind of men we're dealing with here. And they ain't the kind you just up and let go."

Joshua had a puzzled look about him. "You want to expound on that, like them educated fellers say?" he said.

"Sure. Remember Pa saying he couldn't figure out what Vegas meant by claiming he had a professional interest in our prisoners?"

"Yeah."

"Did it ever strike you that thievery and stealing might just be the *profession* he was hinting at?"

His eyes got wide, as though he'd just brought in the mother lode up in Virginia City. "By God, you might have something there, Chance. You just might. And if those fellers don't know Terrence and his men, why, they might just be recruiting 'em."

I gave Jack Terrence a glance, not caring whether he heard my words or not. "These fellas would sure be obliged to Vegas and his men if they got out too," I said.

"You can't find anything good about us, can you, Carston?" Terrence said, a bit of mad showing.

"It's hard, Terrence, real hard."

There was a knock on the back door. I had my Colt's in hand and was moving toward the door before

Joshua could make a move. I signaled him to keep an eye on the front of the building. After all, this could be some kind of diversion.

"State your business or git," I said and flattened myself against the wall, just in case whoever it was decided to do some shooting.

"It's me, Chance, Sarah Ann," I heard a high-pitched voice say. Slowly, I opened the door and there she was all right. Sarah Ann was standing there with a basket of food in her arms. Behind her was Big John Porter.

"It's a good thing you got friendly," John said in his gravelly voice. "I'd have kicked that door in if you hadn't." He wasn't in any too friendly a mood and walked right past his son without saying a word. But then, I didn't hear Jack Terrence make an offering either. I'd hate to be in between the two of them when they got into a fight.

"I brought you all some food," Sarah Ann said, and began to pass plates with fried potatoes and sandwiches made of thick slices of roast beef. There was enough for all six of us. Joshua got out some extra cups and Big John poured the coffee.

"Got a bone to pick, do you, John?" I asked Sarah Ann's father as she dished out the food. He was still wearing his apron. What put him a mite out of place was the oversize Colt's Dragoon horse pistol he had sticking in the belt around his waist. The Dragoon was too big for a normal man to carry as a belt gun, so a saddle holster had been designed for it and it had been the official cavalryman's horse pistol from the Mexican War to the beginning of the War Between the States. But Big John Porter could heft it like I did the

Colt's Army Model .44, so to ask him why he carried such a handgun was folly. I had a notion he likely had an old Walker Colt's, an even heavier model, stuck away in his trunk if he ever figured he was going to get in some real trouble.

"I saw 'em take Will and your brother," John said. "I guess I'm just tired of cleaning up my boy's messes." He looked back at his son, gave him a hateful glare.

"That ain't fair, Pa," Jack Terrence said, a hurt look about him. "It ain't fair and you know it."

"He's right, Papa," Sarah Ann said. "I can only remember a little bit about having Jack around when I was young. But you ain't being fair to him."

Big John Porter was like a lot of men in that if he didn't get his own way, he ignored the subject, figuring it would go away. Ignoring his son and daughter and their accusations was how he was handling this situation. Me, I wasn't going to tell him how to run his life. Not hardly!

"What do they want?" John said, looking out the door.

"Exchange Pa and Wash for our prisoners," I said. "But I'm wondering if these yahoos don't have a price on their heads."

"You just may be right, Chance," Joshua said. "Why, I remember reading just recent that there was a train robbery back in Ohio a few months back. A train, can you believe it! Now, that's brassy! You just wait till them railroads get out here. Why they'll be robbing them too!"

"They're a brazen bunch, all right," John agreed. "That's your brother and pa in there, Chance. You got any recommendations? I reckon it's you who ought to have the last say in this matter."

"Fact of the matter is, I do, John," I said. I didn't say anything more for a minute, instead rifled Pa's desk until I found what I was looking for. It purely surprised them when they saw it. But I felt a real sense of pride when I hefted that Texas Ranger badge in my hand and felt a chill go down my spine. Mind you, the Texas Rangers had been disbanded during the War Between the States, and I'd only put the badge on once since I'd come back, that being when we went out after Ma's killers.

"Here, Chance," Sarah Ann said. "Let me put it on you." She proceeded to pin the badge right over my vest pocket, which felt real familiar, even though it had been some years now.

"I figure it's about time these fellas find out that they're dealing with Texas Rangers," I said with a good deal of pride, and if it showed, well, I felt right good about it.

"Too bad Weatherby ain't here," Joshua said.

"Why's that?"

"He'd tell you you couldn't do this 'cause the rangers don't exist no more," he said with a smile.

"Joshua, with all the tact Weatherby and Wright may have, they just ain't found out a thing or two yet."

"What's that, Chance?"

"Pa always said that you can't stop a good man who's in the right."

"Now you've got the idea," John Porter said and checked the loads of his Colt's Dragoon.

CHAPTER

★ 22 ★

I rifled through Pa's desk again until I found a spare cylinder for my Colt's. I knew there was a second gun and a spare cylinder in the saddlebags of my horse, but the horse was in front of the jail, and walking out front wasn't the healthiest thing a body could do at the moment.

"I still don't know how they come this way," I said, more to myself than anyone else. "I mean, hearing gossip in town is one thing, but how'd they come to pick this town?" While the words came out, I double-checked my weapons.

"If you're as big a hero as Sarah Ann claims Wash is making you out to be, it might just be that you

Carstons got you a bit of a reputation while you was south of the border," Big John said. It threw me to hear that my younger brother was talking me up the way he apparently was. I suddenly gave myself one more reason to get Wash out of this mess. A man can always find use for a body who thinks highly of him. If you know what I mean.

"Could be, John," I said. I knew that the gossip in those small Mexican towns spread like wildfire. It would be the perfect place for Lucy, our own town gossip, to live. A paradise, for sure. With strangers wandering through town, why, the gossip would travel that much faster. The trouble was that a good deal of those strangers were men in the wrong line of work. If Vegas did indeed know the law, like he claimed, and heard of our presence in the area, tracking us north would make sense. Besides, a man like Vegas would know that there was more money in the banks of Texas than he would find in the treasury of Mexico. At least until this fight between Juarez and Maximilian was over with.

"You're probably right," I decided.

"How do you want to do this?" John asked.

"Well, if we head out the front, they're gonna shoot us down like sitting ducks," I said. "Might be time to put those lessons I learned in the war to use."

"How's that?" Joshua said, still keeping watch out the front window.

"Flanking movements, I reckon," I said. "We can go out the back door and spread out on each side."

"Sounds good," John said.

"What do you want me to do, Chance?" Joshua said. "I hope you ain't fixing to leave me out of this."

192

"Not hardly," was my reply. I took a gander out the front window, trying to figure out how we could pull this off. "Pa's gonna be madder than a wet hen when he hears that glass breaking all to hell and gone."

"Come again?" Joshua said with a squint.

"You see that big bay window in the front of the saloon?"

"Sure," Joshua said, then realized what I had in mind. "Say, wait a minute, Chance. You ain't thinking what I think you're thinking, are you?"

"Most likely." I smiled.

"Why, if I shoot that window out, your daddy is gonna have me start working somewhere on the other side of the state!"

"You leave Pa to me, Joshua."

"It's a deal."

If Joshua was worried, he had all the reason in the world to be so. Since I'd been back I'd found out that Pa had placed great pride on the fact that a good deal of the buildings in town had glass windows, including the saloon. Mind you now, plate glass was hard to come by. All the way from Saint Louis, if what Pa had said was right. It was expensive too. But right now the whole town could have been made of glass and I wouldn't have cared less. Hell, that was my kin they had inside the saloon, and getting them back safe and sound was the only thing in my mind. Everything else was expendable, just like it had been in the army.

"What's the idea of shooting out the window?" John asked.

"The way I figure it, John, by the time we try breaking down the front doors, they could unload on us something fierce," I said. "If Joshua can shoot out that window, why, I figure a big man like you can step right into the saloon with no trouble at all." It must have made sense to the big man, 'cause he nodded silently. "I'll be right there with you when we do it," I added as a bit of comfort.

"Say, what if you boys get stuck in there?" Joshua asked.

"Then I reckon you get to save us all by your lonesome, Joshua," I said.

I picked up one of Pa's Remingtons and had my Colt's still in its holster as I started toward the back door. Jack Terrence reached out and grabbed hold of my left arm.

"You got to let us loose, damn it!" he said, the bully in him showing now. It didn't last for long.

"Let go of my arm or I'll kill you here and now, Terrence," I said through gritted teeth as I stuck the Remington in his chest.

"If he doesn't, I will," came the gravelly sound of Big John Porter's voice behind me.

I never did ask and none of the Porters offered an explanation, but I had a notion it was the harsh words his father spoke at him more than the business end of the Remington that made Jack Terrence loosen his grip on my arm. He was a strong man who might have a lot of guts in the right situation, but he couldn't stand up to his father. Big as he was, Jack Terrence Porter would never be able to take his father in anything. But that was something the two would have to straighten out between themselves when there was time.

Right now there wasn't time.

I'd come to the conclusion not long after the war

started that the only people who made a lot of money in any war were the armsmakers. Colt, Remington, Spencer, Henry, take your pick, they all made a good profit from the war. They just had enough sense not to fight the damn war. I smiled to myself as we walked out the back door of the jail.

"Odd time to find something to fun about, ain't it?" John said. I reckon he'd seen my smile.

"I was just thinking," I said. "When the war started, Sam Colt knew he was gonna make money hand over fist with this new pistol." I patted the Colt's New Model Army Revolver at my side. "He knew there was a war coming, so he called these things his 'latest work in moral reform.' "

"Moral reform?" I had him stumped.

"Wouldn't you call getting rid of Vegas and his like moral reform?" I said with a smile.

John smiled back. "Yeah, I guess you're right."

We split up, John heading one way, me the other, dodging the alleyways about two buildings on either side of the jail. Joshua was going to give us about five minutes to get in place alongside the main street. When we were set, Joshua would use close to a full magazine of that Henry of his, trying to break out that window and keep anyone from seeing us cross the street in the process.

That was the plan, anyway.

I made it to my position with no problem and only hoped Big John had found his place that easy. After all, just because I'd counted nine of these yahoos in front of Kelly's Hardware earlier didn't mean there might not be more of them hidden in various parts of the town. No sir.

195

I let Joshua get off about two well-placed shots before I ran like the very devil. Glass splattered all over the place as I saw John take gigantic strides across his side of the street. If I'd made a more exact count, I would have sworn the man only took six or eight huge steps. But like I say, they were *huge* steps.

I'll tell you something else that was strange sprinting across that street, hoss. I'd have sworn I saw a woman out of the corner of my eye, but when I glanced again she wasn't there. Maybe I was just getting too excited.

Big John made it to the saloon side of the street as easily as I did. We both began working our way toward the saloon, as Joshua eased up his firing. I was about ten feet from the door of the saloon when Joshua let out three quick shots and one of the yahoos inside fell out the window, lifeless as could be. I made a mental note to tell Joshua that I thought he was a whale of a shot with that Henry rifle of his, when this thing was all over.

But it wasn't over yet.

Suddenly, everything went quiet. Or at least the gunfire stopped. Big John squinted at me, as curious as I was as to what was going on inside, if anything. Had they gone? Did they pack up and turn tail and run? Were Pa and Wash inside? More importantly, were they alive? I was hoping the same thoughts were running through John Porter's mind, for I didn't know how much longer I could stand the suspense. After all, Pa and Wash were good friends of John's.

"Nuts," I muttered, half to myself and half to anyone else who might want to listen. Then I pulled out my Colt's and, with both guns in hand, leaped in front of the window, hoping I could find something to shoot at before jumping inside. Big John took one big step from his side of the window and did the same, squinting. He only had that Dragoon in his hand, but I reckon that was all he figured he'd need.

"Look out!" I heard Pa yell from back and to the side of the saloon. I couldn't see anyone but Pa and Wash and a man standing guard over them. But he was enough. The man swung his rifle butt and hit Pa a glancing blow to the side of the head, knocking him off the chair he was seated on. It was the last thing the guard did.

I shot the son of a bitch. Dead.

"Pa, are you all right?" I said, taking a step inside the saloon. Wash was leaning over Pa now, worried about his wound. Hell, I was beginning to worry too.

It was a big mistake.

"Don't move, Carston," I heard Vegas say. By the time I saw him standing in back of the bar, he had three other men with him and every one of them had a pistol or a rifle trained on me.

Damn but I felt like a fool.

CHAPTER
★ 23 ★

Drop the guns if you want to stay healthy," another of the men said from the shadows of the corner, near the front door. I took a quick glance around, saw the odds were stacked against me, and tossed the pistols on a table nearby. All the while I could feel the blood rushing to my face, for I felt embarrassed as hell. Not to mention mad.

Then I remembered something Pa had told us time and again over the years. "Mad will win more fights than anything else in the world," was what he'd say. Me, I was getting mad.

"Get away from him," the outlaw in the corner said,

as he strolled across the floor and all but kicked Wash away from Pa, who was bleeding from the side of the head. Mind you, now, I *knew* there were at least four, maybe five guns trained on me and John. But I just didn't care. No sir. No sooner had the man kicked my brother than I was taking some mighty long strides across the room.

"Hey!" Vegas yelled. I reckon he was talking to me. Or maybe he was going to warn his friend. Either way, I made it work for me. The guard turned around about the same time Wash was scrambling to his feet. It wasn't the first time that Wash and I had actually worked together instead of fighting one another. Believe me, my brother knew the look of rage that could fill my eyes. Hell, he'd seen it often enough in his youth. So he knew what was coming. He stuck his foot out in back of the guard while I landed a hard right to the man's jaw. To say that he flipped ass over teakettle would be putting it lightly. He dropped like a piece of bulk lead. In so doing, he cracked his head against the floor, knocking himself out from the blow.

"Smart ass," I growled.

"Are you looking to die?" Vegas asked, an incredulous look on his face. I reckon he couldn't believe what I had just done.

"I never met a man who wanted to die, mister," I said. "But you mistreat my family the way you have, and I reckon I will get ready to die. That's a fact." My words weren't hard or complicated. They were the simple truth. Hell, I'd have said the very same thing to the devil himself.

Big John Porter had tossed his gun on the table. But

you could tell he wasn't any too scared either. "You know, you boys oughtta give up right now, instead of causing any more fuss than you have."

Vegas and his men, and me too, for that matter, gave him a stare. If Joshua thought Vegas taking over the saloon was brassy, he should have heard Big John Porter's words that afternoon! "We got you surrounded, you know."

Vegas let out a laugh, which was soon followed by those of his men, who did the same.

"You people are crazy," Vegas muttered in disbelief. Good, I thought to myself, maybe that will keep him confused a mite.

Wash was getting that killing look in his own eyes now, more for what had happened to Pa, I thought, than for any hatred he might have had for these outlaws.

"Take it easy, Wash," I said in a lowered voice. "These fellas just think we're crazy. They ain't even aware of how deadly we can be." It gave my brother reason to pause and, I hoped, the knowledge that I hadn't given up on getting us out of there alive.

"How's Will?" John asked, looking down on Wash and me, who were already leaning over Pa.

"Don't be crowding him," another outlaw said. John stepped back, but neither Wash nor I moved as I took off my neckerchief and dabbed at Pa's head wound.

"Here, I'll do that," Wash said. "Give me some water and a bottle of that whiskey," he added to anyone who was listening, still concentrating on Pa.

"Huh?" the nearest outlaw said.

"Are you deaf, dumb, or what?" Wash said, giving

the man a look that said he was getting as mad as me. It made the man jump, I'll say that.

If Wash could take care of Pa, I figured it was time to think about how we were going to get out of here alive. There were five of these pilgrims that I counted in sight, including Vegas. Like everybody else I'd seen of late, they were armed to hunt bear at least. Six-guns, rifles, knives, the whole lot of it. Fact of the matter is, it was a good thing I took in what I did too, for it jogged my mind and gave me a new bit of hope. Yes sir.

"How are you doing, Pa?" I said as he opened his eyes and Wash poured a mite of whiskey down his gullet. Pa coughed a bit and I gave him a pat on the back. When I did, I knew we still had hope, or at least some semblance of hope.

Most folks don't realize that there are weapons all around them. They take to looking for rifles and pistols and bowie knives, obvious things like that which hang on a man. I'd gotten so excited of late that I'd almost forgotten the Tinker knife that Pa had hanging down his back. It was a balanced throwing knife that Pa had made for himself some years back. I'd never seen him use it all that much, but it was patting him on the back like I did that brought back the memory.

"You get through babying your old man, boy, you can get up against the wall with him," Vegas said. He had too much confidence about him, more like he was enjoying being a smart ass than a knowing man. I didn't like it, not one bit.

"I wouldn't go pushing that man, mister," John said. "I wouldn't say that you'll live to regret it, but as long as you live, you'll regret it. I guarantee that." Big John gave Vegas a wink and a nod.

"You know, I've about had it with you people," Vegas said, his smile and confidence suddenly turned to downright anger. "I am nice to you but all you do is mouth off." He made a big mistake then.

Vegas walked up to Big John and decided to show him who was running the place. He slapped John across the mouth, likely as hard as he could. Oh, you could hear the flesh meet flesh, ringing out as loud as could be, but John's face didn't move. Not one inch.

That was Vegas's mistake. But by the time he recognized it, it was too late. He was too surprised at hitting an immovable mountain to see John's hand come up alongside his head. But he felt it all right. Like John said, I guarantee it. Believe me, any man who gets thrown into the side of a wooden chair and breaks it up as hard and fast as Vegas did, well, hoss, he felt it.

There was total silence in the room as Vegas came to and dusted himself off. There was no doubt he didn't like what had happened to him. Seeing the revenge in his eyes, I knew the end wasn't far off.

"You'll die for that!" he hissed at John.

"Not before you do." The voice was as strong and hard as the last time I'd heard it, but it was totally unexpected. "Saving your ass again, Chance," Ben said from the back of the room.

All attention had turned to Ben now, and well it might, for the man had a shotgun in his hands and an expression on his face that said he wasn't too pleased with what these fellows had done to his friends.

Wash had gotten Pa up to a sitting position and onto

a chair. It looked like the odds were getting better so I stood behind the chair, placing my hands on Pa's shoulders. Like everyone else, I had my eyes on Ben now.

"Got twenty miles toward Matamoras before I realized I'd left my shotgun up here for fixing when I took off with you boys," Ben said.

"I'm glad you come back, Ben," Pa said, rubbing his head. "Although I don't know as you picked the right time."

Ben smiled, taking in the outlaws before him. "Oh, it was the right time, all right." Everything went silent for a few moments then before Ben squinted at me as though I were daft. "Good Lord, boy, is that a ranger badge you're wearing?"

"A ranger badge?" Vegas said in disbelief. I reckon he'd been too wrapped up in his own doings to notice it until now. But after close examination, he broke out into laughter. "Would you look at that, boys. A ranger badge! Why, that's as useless as you, Carston!"

By God, that tore it! I wanted to kill him! And I got my chance, for it wasn't long before all hell broke loose.

"Now, son, you don't want to do that," Ben said to one of two men facing him, not ten feet away. The two had begun edging their hands toward their holsters.

Then a giant oak tree busted down the front door to the saloon and got everyone's attention! The oak tree was Jack Terrence, who looked about as mad as his father. He had a six-gun in his hand and fired at the first man he saw, hitting him in the chest, but not before the man had put a rifle slug in Terrence's own chest.

Big John was going for his Dragoon when Vegas made his move. But it wasn't John that Vegas fired at. He was turning toward the door as he did, and placed two shots in Jack Terrence's stomach, doubling the man up as he fell to the floor.

I pulled the Tinker knife out of the sheath down Pa's back and threw it hard. It hit Vegas in the side of the neck, busting a vein hard enough to send blood gushing all over the place. But Big John was used to blood, so he kept on moving in one motion as he cocked and fired his Dragoon twice into Vegas. They were both chest wounds that did the gang leader in before he hit the floor.

If Big John's Dragoon was loud, Ben's shotgun was louder. The blast of the first barrel visibly lifted one of his opponents off the floor, putting a lot more blood and guts into the air. I thought I saw some blood wet Ben's shirt near his side as the second man fired, only to receive the second barrel full of buckshot for his efforts and die the same way his partner had.

A man not far from us had leveled his pistol at the three of us and shot Pa, who fell to the floor. His second shot hit me in the shoulder and it hurt like hell, but I determined that he was a dead man, no matter what happened next. You don't kill my Pa and get away with it for too awful long. Moral reform, my ass! I was going to kill the son of a bitch!

Like I said, Wash makes up for not being heavy with being fast, and he was the first one to the culprit, but not for long. The man still had his pistol in hand and, even though Wash had pinned his back against the bar, he brought the sharp end of the butt down on my brother's head, giving him a wound not unlike Pa's.

I rushed him and he kicked me in the stomach, doubling me over. I looked up and he was cocking his six-gun, readying to kill me. Somehow, I had to get him. He couldn't get away with this. No!

He never made it.

A rifle shot sent echoes through the place and the would-be killer slumped to the floor, dead. I was just getting my senses back when I saw Joshua standing in the doorway, gunsmoke swirling out of the barrel of his Henry.

"Looks like I had to come over and save you all by my lonesome," he said, "just like you said."

"Yeah." I wanted to thank him a whole lot more, but the thought of what had happened to Pa filled me now and gunshot or not I made my way to him.

I never have understood why a lawman was supposed to wear his badge over the left side of his chest the way he does. Maybe it was to make a good target for those figuring to do him in, maybe it was to protect him. In Pa's case, I reckon it did both. He was only half-conscious when I got to him, and the pain in my shoulder told me I knew what he must have been feeling. Or so I thought.

"Did you know you're bleeding, Chance?" Wash asked, surprised.

"Yeah. Son of a bitch shot me in the same place the old wound was."

"Looks like Pa's a mite luckier than you." My brother smiled.

"He's alive?" This time I was the one with the incredulous look on my face. "Thank God," I heard myself mumble under my breath. "How'd he do it?"

"Rosa, I'd say," Wash said and really had me

puzzled. My brother had torn open Pa's shirt and had his bowie knife ready to perform some kind of quick surgery. You get real good at that out here. But he hadn't had to do much digging at all. It seems the bullet had gone through a good portion of Pa's badge and would have come close to killing him. But Pa had Rosa's small box containing the rosary she had given him when we'd left Mexico. The bullet was only partially lodged in his chest. In fact, it almost looked like you could pick it out with your fingers! "Way I figure it, he's likely got some beads and maybe part of that rosary stuck in him behind that bullet, but it ain't nowhere close to his heart. Besides," he added, smiling at Pa, "he's too tough to die."

Pa smiled back and said, "How's Jack Terrence?"

I'd forgotten clean about the man who had saved us from this bunch. My whole side was warm with blood now, but I made it over to Jack who now lay dying I was sure. I picked up my Colt's and holstered it on the way over to him. You learn to get real cautious about things out here. Yes sir.

Jack Terrence wouldn't last out the day, of that I was sure. His face had drained and even a big man like him was feeling nothing but pain with the three slugs he had in him now. Sarah Ann had appeared from nowhere and was kneeling beside him, as was Big John. She was crying. Big John, well, the look on his face might have been that of a small boy rather than a grown man.

"I never rode with Quantrill, Pa," Jack Terrence said. I had a notion he wanted to set something straight with his last words. He did. "It was rumors that got started. I just let 'em be. Only made folks hate me the more."

"We don't hate you, Jack," his sister said through her tears. "Do we, Papa?" I couldn't tell whether it was a question or a statement, but Sarah Ann looking up at her papa the way she did demanded an answer.

"No, Jack, we don't hate you," John said. "I never did hate you, son, I just never understood you." Jack Terrence smiled at Big John. I could tell it was something he'd waited to hear for a long time. "I killed the one who shot you, you know," John added after a pause.

Jack Terrence smiled again, if forced. With as much pain as he was feeling, I knew he didn't have long. "I knew you would. I knew if I could force their hand—"

He never finished, for he died speaking those words. I thought I saw a tear come to Big John Porter's face so I looked away. I knew he'd find time to do his own grieving in private.

"Did you let all of 'em out?" I asked Joshua.

"Wasn't my idea," he said. "Miss Sarah Ann suggested it."

"Where'd the rest of 'em go?" I asked.

I didn't have to wait for an answer, for I heard a good deal of gunfire erupt out on the streets and somehow knew it was them.

CHAPTER
★ 24 ★

Wash," I said, getting up and heading for the shot-out window of the saloon. My left shoulder hurt like hell, but I could still use my right side, which was my shooting side. I had my Colt's in my hand by the time I'd stepped out through the bay window. In a split second, Wash was there beside me.

"What's going on?" he asked excitedly.

"Is that Garver and Quartermain?" I said, seeing two men with six-guns across the street approaching the bank. My first thought was that they were about to rob the bank, and by God, I had money in that bank! Jack Terrence might have turned out to be a good man, but I was having real fast second thoughts about his partners.

"Sure does," my brother said, checking the loads of his new toy, the LeMat pistol. "You think—"

"Wait a minute," I interrupted, and did some quick figures in my head. "Were there five of those men in the saloon?"

"Yeah." Then it hit Wash as quick as it had me. "You mean—"

"Sure as God made green apples." I nodded. The remaining four men in Vegas's bunch had taken to robbing our bank while we were having a shoot-out with the rest of their gang!

A shot rang out inside the bank. What followed was a lot more gunplay, as the four men burst out of the bank, two of them carrying flour sacks, no doubt filled with our money. They could have been watching the horses, but I had a notion that Garver and Quartermain must have seen these men go into the bank and waited for them to come out, for they didn't join them. Instead, they got off two shots, hitting two men, but only wounding them. The two men not carrying money bags riddled Garver and Quartermain with bullets. The undertaker was going to get a lot of business today, of that I was sure.

Then Abigail Cross ran out of the bank and yelled *"Stop"* as loud as she could. One of the men Garver and Quartermain had wounded simply turned to Abigail and shot her dead. If there is one thing the Western men have a good deal of respect for, it is their women. You don't do anything to them without getting some kind of revenge put on you. I shot that son of a bitch in the head, putting him out of his misery.

The bank robbers were running for their horses, which were just outside the bank. But Wash put a quick stop to that. He flipped a switch on that LeMat pistol of his and let fly a whole bunch of buckshot, which hit both the horses and the men. All of a sudden the men of the town were coming out of the doors of the various stores, as Wash and me shot our way across the street.

One of the robbers tried to hide between two horses, but we fixed him right quick. Wash shot his legs out from under him, and when he fell to the ground and the horses moved away, I shot him twice more. They were fatal shots that assured the undertaker of one more customer.

Hubert Weatherby stepped out of a store and, with one quick blast, shotgunned a third outlaw to death. Didn't even get that fancy suit of his dirty in the doing of it.

The one remaining outlaw had a sack full of money and had managed to find a horse that wasn't bucking. He rode low in the saddle as he tried to get out of town. Jason Wright was at the north end of town and was ready to stop the man, but wasn't quick enough. He held an old Spencer up but before he could get a shot off, the outlaw killed him where he stood.

I knew Wash's LeMat was no good at that range, so I took a bead on the man's back and fired. Not a second later I heard a report from a rifle that came from the area of the saloon. I knew my shot had hit the rider in the small of the back. It was when he threw up his hands that I knew Ben had nailed him for good with a shot from a Henry rifle, which he slowly handed back to Joshua.

"What happened to all that civilization you were bragging about?" I asked Weatherby.

"To hell with civilization!" the man said in a rage. "These bastards were stealing the money out of our bank!"

People were gathering around the bodies of Abigail Cross and Jason Wright, who would never know wedded bliss. It was too bad. I thought they would have enjoyed that life. But then, dying seemed to be the order of the day.

"What about that Vegas character and all the shooting in the saloon?" Weatherby asked, seeing the wound I sported.

"Vegas should have stuck with his law books. He damn sure wasn't any good with a gun," was all I said.

"Taught 'em not to tangle with a ranger, did you?" Weatherby said with a proud smile.

I looked down at the Texas Ranger badge that was now smeared with blood and reminded myself I had also been shot.

"Yeah," I half chuckled to myself.

Suddenly, I felt very tired. All I wanted to do was find a place to sit down and have someone take this damn bullet out of me. The way my shoulder felt now, I doubted if it would ever heal.

CHAPTER
★ 25 ★

You never saw so many people get to bragging about the men of their town like the citizens of Twin Rifles for about a week after that shoot-out. They couldn't talk enough about how the Carstons and Porters, and even Ben and Weatherby and the men Pa had jailed had come to the aid of the town when they were called upon. No one brought up the matter of Pa losing his job, although I doubted that was ever a possibility. Pa just had too much respect from these people to have them turn on him like Weatherby had once claimed they would.

Ben stuck around and had his day of glory, he and

Joshua toting badges while Pa and I got over our wounds. Pa's wound had been a bit bizarre to the doctor, who pulled out a couple of beads of a rosary from Pa's wound. Someone said he almost got religion. Me, I was back to nursing a bad shoulder that had gotten worse, and I don't mind telling you it wasn't the best time I've ever had in my life.

It took close to four days before they got everyone buried. It wasn't the undertaker, you understand, as much as it was the digging of the graves for everyone. Except for Vegas, no one knew the names of any of the rest of his group, so I wasn't surprised about the way they buried them. I walked past the marker that spoke for the fate of all of them the third day after the shooting. I had just been to the funeral for Abigail Cross and Jason Wright, who had been buried together. It seemed only right.

The sign wasn't like any cross you'd ever find in a graveyard, but it said all that needed saying:

HERE LIES VEGAS
AND HIS EIGHT FRIENDS.
GUNMEN AND THIEVES
WHO RODE INTO THE WRONG TOWN.
THEIR TRAIL ENDS HERE.

Pa and I got better and, at the end of a week, decided to see what Margaret and Rachel Ferris were up to.

"Say, Margaret," Pa said one morning as she poured him some after-breakfast coffee. Neither one of us had lost our appetite, no matter how severe the wounds.

"Yes, Will."

"You know, woman, you've got a right pretty smile," Pa said.

"Careful, Will, you're flirting," Margaret said with a smile.

"Me and Chance was talking. You know how you was talking some time back about being appreciated?" Pa said in a fairly uncomfortable manner. I had a notion he would rather face down a panther than make a proposition to a woman. But then, who am I to speak, for I felt the same way.

"I seem to recall a conversation like that, yes." She had a twinkle in her eye now, and unless I was wrong, why, she'd be telling Pa to tuck in his shirttail before long.

"What he's trying to say, Miss Margaret, is that if you ladies would care to close down your eatery for the afternoon and fix a mite of take along food, why, me and Pa would like to escort you down to that shady spot by the creek."

Rachel had walked out from the kitchen as I spoke. "Does that mean we've got to put up with you being mean as can be?"

"No, ma'am," I said. "As long as you don't steal my horses, why, I'll be nice as can be."

The women suggested that Wash see if Sarah Ann would like to join us that afternoon. She did and the women spent the morning cooking up fried chicken and some other extras that went along with the meal.

But Pa wasn't about to eat a meal without coffee if it was available, so he took some Arbuckles and our old coffeepot along for good measure that afternoon.

We had a good time of it that afternoon. Yes, we did.

It was when Pa got the urge for some coffee that he sent me and Wash out to hunt up some firewood. I was looking down at the ground for the deadwood or I would have noticed him riding up on me slow, like he did. Or maybe I was thinking of Rachel and didn't even hear him. But all of a sudden I looked up and there was Ben on his horse.

"I told you you'd come back," he said with a smile, seeing the women over by the creek. "Man would be a damn fool not to."

"Yeah, I reckon so."

"Women take the rough out of a man." It was true enough, but I didn't particularly want to talk about how I felt about a woman with Ben.

"What're you doing out here?" I asked.

"Well, I got my shotgun and you boys seem like you can handle things right well again. I figured I'd be moving on. Maybe try finding Shelby again," he said.

"I wish you luck, Ben," I said.

"Man can always use that." He smiled. He was silent for a moment, maybe feeling as awkward as I was, before he snapped his fingers. "Oh, yeah, I near forgot. Joshua said he got word back that Vegas was a wanted man. I don't know about those yahoos he was with, but he had a decent amount of money on his head. Old Weatherby wanted to give it to me because I shot that last fella out of his saddle and saved some of the bank's money."

"Must not have heard my Colt's go off," I said. "You gonna have 'em forward the money to you? Now that you're leaving and all?"

"Actually, I told Joshua to put it in your account in that bank."

"My account?"

"Hell, yes," Ben said. "Shoot, Chance, you stopped that man as much as I did. Besides, this is your town. Your country." He slowly looked about him, taking in the land he was leaving, knowing, I suspected, that it would get much worse the farther south he headed. And drier, much drier.

"How much money was on his head?" I asked.

"Four hundred dollars."

"Lordy," I said and gave a low whistle.

"Ben, I've got to ask you one thing. I've got to know before you leave," I said.

Ben shrugged. "I'll answer it if I can."

"What the devil is your name? I mean besides Ben?"

"Now, why would you have to know that, Chance?"

"You're too handy a man to know on just a first name basis," I said, hoping it would serve as justification.

He scratched his head, squinted, looked around as though half the Comanche nation might be lurking, and leaned over his horse toward me. "How good are you at keeping it under your hat, if I tell you, Chance?"

"Sure," I said. "I understand. The law and all. It's a deal."

"Thompson," he said. "Ben Thompson."

I stuck out a paw and he took it. "Well, Ben Thompson, it's been nice having you to ride the river with."

"It does get rough, doesn't it?" He laughed.

Then he was gone, saying his short good-byes to the women and Pa and heading south.

"I wonder who he is, Chance?" Wash said, watching Ben ride away.

"Just a drifter, passing through, brother," I said. "Let's get that firewood for Pa."

Still, I couldn't help but ask myself the same question my brother had just posed as I watched our friend ride off. Ben Thompson, man killer, was all that ran through my mind. Then I shrugged and began looking for that firewood.

You meet the damnedest people out here.

Like Fighting Jo Shelby.

And Ben Thompson.